AF409414

TANEQUA CROSBY

*S*TRENGTH *B*EYOND *F*LAMES

TANEQUA CROSBY | MITCHELL CROSBY

Dedication

For the ones who've felt the weight of every choice, and for those who have dared to keep going, even when the world seemed heavy.

This story is for you—to remind you of the strength within, the power of brotherhood, and the courage it takes to stand up and keep moving forward. May you always find the light to guide you and know you're never alone on the journey.

Author's Note

Writing this story was a journey close to my heart. It was inspired by the resilience of young people facing life's toughest challenges and by my husband, a firefighter whose bravery and dedication to service motivated me deeply. His work—and the impact he makes every day—is a powerful reminder of how strength and compassion can change lives.

This book is a tribute to the power of community, mentorship, and the choices that shape our paths. For those who have ever felt lost or alone, or struggled to find their way, may this story offer a reminder that there is always hope, someone who believes in you, and a way forward.

Thank you for sharing in this journey.

Table of Contents

Chapter I 1

Chapter II 7

Chapter III 14

Chapter IV 22

Chapter V 30

Chapter VI 35

Chapter VII 40

Chapter VIII 45

Chapter IX 50

Chapter X 57

Chapter XI 64

Chapter XII 70

Chapter XIII 75

Chapter XIV 82

Chapter XV 87

Chapter XVI 93

Chapter XVII *99*

Chapter XVIII *104*

Chapter XIX..*110*

Chapter XX..*114*

Chapter XXI..*118*

Chapter XXII..*123*

Chapter XXIII..*127*

Chapter XXIV *132*

STRENGTH BEYOND FLAMES

Chapter I

The sun was just beginning to rise, casting a warm glow over the fire station as Benjamin Bennett—Ben, to everyone who knew him—inspected the engines. The familiar sound of the engine humming and the scent of gasoline and soot filled the air, mixing with the aroma of fresh coffee brewing inside. Ben relished these quiet moments before the hustle and bustle of the day began.

He had spent the night on call, but now, as he prepared to clock out, something was weighing heavily on his mind. His shift had been uneventful, but he couldn't shake the feeling of unease about the neighborhood surrounding the station. As a firefighter, he often saw the aftermath of violence and despair, and lately, he had been noticing a troubling trend: a group of young boys, teenagers around 15 and 16, hanging around the corners of their community instead of attending school. They laughed and played, but Ben couldn't ignore the potential dangers they faced—the gang violence, drugs, and negative influences lurking just beyond their laughter.

After completing his tasks at the station, Ben decided to stop by his wife Raquel's bakery before heading home. The smell of freshly baked bread and pastries greeted him as he entered, instantly lifting his spirits. Raquel was behind the counter, expertly icing cupcakes. Her face lit up as she saw him. "Hey, love! How was your shift?"

"It was quiet, which is a good thing, I suppose," Ben replied, leaning over the counter to kiss her. "But there's something I need to talk to you about."

Raquel noticed the seriousness in his tone and wiped her hands on her apron, giving him her full attention. "What's going on?"

He took a deep breath, glancing around to ensure no one was within earshot. "I've been seeing some kids hanging out near the station—skipping school, not doing anything productive. It worries me. I feel like I should do something to help them."

Raquel nodded, her expression shifting to concern. "I've seen those boys too. They're so young. What do you have in mind?"

"I want to start a mentorship program," he said, his voice growing more confident. "I think if I can connect with them, show them a different path, it might make a difference. They need someone to believe in them."

Raquel placed a hand on his arm, her support palpable. "That's an amazing idea, Ben. You have the perfect experience for it. But how will you go about it?"

"I'm not sure yet. I think I need to talk to Chief and see what he thinks," Ben replied.

"That sounds like a good start," Raquel said, her eyes sparkling with encouragement. "Just remember to be patient with them. They've probably been through a lot."

Ben nodded, taking in her words. "You're right. It won't be easy, but I can't just sit back and watch them fall into the wrong crowd. I need to make an effort."

After a few more moments of discussion, Ben finished his coffee and prepared to leave. As he stepped outside, he couldn't shake the sense of urgency that had settled in his chest. He needed to make this happen, and soon.

As he quickly went back to the fire station, he parked the truck and took a moment to collect his thoughts. He wanted to ensure his plan was solid before discussing it with his chief. He headed into the office, where Chief Thompson sat at his desk, reviewing reports.

"Hey, Chief, do you have a minute?" Ben asked, trying to keep his tone casual.

"Of course, Ben. What's on your mind?" Chief Thompson looked up, curious.

"I want to start a mentorship program for some of the kids in the neighborhood," Ben began. He explained his observations and the conversations he'd had with Raquel about the boys he'd seen. "I think if we can connect with them, we can steer them away from a dangerous path."

Chief Thompson leaned back in his chair, considering Ben's words. "That's a commendable idea, Ben. We need more programs that focus on community engagement. But you'll need to get approval first."

"I understand. I'd like to speak with the principal at the high school. I think they can help me identify the kids who need the most support," Ben suggested.

"Sounds good. Go ahead and set up a meeting. I'll support you in any way I can," Chief Thompson replied, a hint of pride in his voice.

Ben felt a surge of gratitude. "Thanks, Chief. I appreciate that."

With a plan forming in his mind, Ben left the chief's office feeling hopeful. He grabbed his phone and called the nearby high school, reaching the principal's secretary. "Hi, this is Ben Bennett from the fire department down the street. I'd like to speak with Principal Harris about starting a mentorship program for at-risk youth."

After a brief hold, the secretary returned with a confirmation. "Principal Harris is not available right now, but can meet with you tomorrow afternoon at two o'clock."

"Perfect! Thank you," Ben replied, excitement bubbling within him.

As he drove home, his mind raced with possibilities. He envisioned meeting the kids, forming bonds with them, and helping them navigate their challenges. He couldn't wait to get started.

Later that evening, as Ben and Raquel sat on the porch watching the sunset, he shared his plans for the mentorship program. The golden hues of dusk illuminated their faces, and Raquel listened intently, offering insights and encouragement.

"I believe in you, Ben," she said softly, squeezing his hand. "You have the heart and the experience to make a real difference."

Ben looked at her, gratitude filling his heart. "Thanks, Raq. I hope I can live up to that."

With determination burning within him, he felt ready to take on this new challenge—ready to become the change he wanted to see in the community.

Chapter II

The morning sun streamed through the kitchen window, casting a warm glow on the table where Raquel was busy preparing breakfast. The scent of sizzling bacon filled the air, mingling with the aroma of freshly brewed coffee. Ben sat at the table with a notepad in front of him, jotting down ideas for his mentorship program. The excitement from the previous day's conversation still lingered in his mind, fueling his determination.

"Are you ready for your meeting with Principal Harris?" Raquel asked, placing a plate of eggs in front of him.

"Yeah, I think so," Ben replied, looking up from his notes. "I've been thinking about what I want to say and how to explain what I envision for the program."

"Just remember to be yourself," Raquel encouraged, pouring him a cup of coffee. "You know what you're doing, and you have the passion to back it up."

Ben smiled at her, grateful for her unwavering support. "Thanks, Raq. I really appreciate you being here for me. It means a lot."

After finishing breakfast, Ben quickly gathered his things and climbed into his truck. He drove to the fire station, his mind racing with thoughts about the mentorship program. Once there, he parked and entered the building, feeling the familiar comfort of the bustling environment.

After clocking in, Ben grabbed a few minutes to prepare for the day. He reviewed his notes, refining his pitch for the program in his mind. A few of his colleagues noticed his focused demeanor.

"Everything alright, Ben?" asked Chris, one of the younger firefighters.

"Yeah, just a big meeting today," Ben replied, trying to maintain his composure. "I'm pitching a mentorship program for some kids in the neighborhood."

"Sounds interesting. Good luck with that!" Chris offered, giving him a thumbs up before heading out for a training drill.

As the clock ticked closer to the meeting time, Ben felt a mix of excitement and nervousness. He knew he had to get this right, not just for himself, but for the boys who would rely on him.

By 1:30 PM, he decided to head to the local high school. The thought of finally meeting the principal filled him with anticipation. He knew that this could be the beginning of something transformative, not just for the boys but for the community as well.

Upon arriving at the school, Ben parked his truck and took a deep breath before stepping inside. The bustling hallways were alive with the sounds of students laughing and chatting. He navigated through the sea of teenagers, reflecting on how much had changed since his own school days.

He made his way to Principal Harris's office, and after a quick knock, he was invited in. The principal was a middle-aged man with a friendly demeanor, wearing glasses that slipped down his nose as he reviewed papers on his desk. He looked up and smiled warmly as Ben entered.

"Mr. Bennett! It's good to see you. I appreciate you coming in," Principal Harris said, extending his hand.

"Thank you for meeting with me, Principal Harris," Ben replied, shaking the man's hand firmly. "I'm excited to discuss the mentorship program I want to start for some of the kids in our community."

"Absolutely. I think it's a wonderful initiative," Principal Harris said, leaning back in his chair. "Tell me more about your vision."

Ben took a deep breath, feeling the weight of the moment. "I've noticed some boys in the neighborhood who seem to be struggling. They're skipping school, and getting involved with the wrong crowd, and I think they need someone to guide them. I want to create a program where I can connect with them, provide mentorship, and show them a better path."

The principal nodded thoughtfully, his expression serious. "That's commendable. We definitely have students who could benefit from your guidance. Do you have specific kids in mind, or are you looking for recommendations?"

"I'd like to work with names you can provide. I don't want to assume who needs help. I'd rather get the input of the school staff who see them every day," Ben explained, his passion evident in his voice.

"Of course, that makes perfect sense," Principal Harris replied. "I can give you a list of students who have been identified as at-risk. They've faced challenges in their lives, and I believe they would greatly benefit from having a mentor like you."

Ben felt a wave of relief wash over him. "Thank you, that would be incredibly helpful."

"I'll put together some names and contact information, and we can set up a meeting with them as soon as you're ready," the principal suggested. "I think it's important for you to meet them, but I also want to ensure they're willing to engage in the program."

"Absolutely," Ben agreed, envisioning the day he would sit down with the boys and discuss their futures.

After their conversation wrapped up, Principal Harris handed Ben a folder containing the names and brief profiles of the students. "Take this home and review it. We can schedule a follow-up meeting to discuss the next steps."

"Thank you, Principal Harris," Ben said, genuinely appreciative of the support.

As he exited the office, a mix of excitement and nervousness swirled within him. This was the moment he had been waiting for—the chance to connect with the boys and make a difference in their lives. He headed back to his truck, eager to get home and review the information.

Once inside the comfort of his vehicle, he opened the folder and scanned the names. Each one represented a story, a challenge, and the possibility of change. As he read through the profiles, he found himself feeling a deeper sense of responsibility. These boys were not just names on a page; they were real people with real struggles.

Ben drove home, the weight of the folder resting in his lap, and his mind racing with ideas for how he could approach the mentorship. He envisioned activities they could do together, conversations they could have, and the bonds he could build. He thought about how he could create a safe space for them to express their fears and aspirations.

Arriving home, he found Raquel in the garden, tending to the flowers. The sight of her calmed his racing thoughts, and he joined her, kneeling beside her in the rich soil.

"Hey, love," she said, glancing up with a smile. "How did it go?"

Ben handed her the folder. "The principal was supportive, and he's going to provide me with names of students who could use mentorship. I'm really excited but also nervous about meeting them."

Raquel opened the folder and skimmed through the profiles. "These boys are lucky to have you, Ben. I can already see how much you care."

"Thanks, Raq. I just hope I can make a real impact. I want them to feel like they can trust me, to know that I believe in them," he said, reflecting on the weight of his responsibility.

"You will, I have no doubt. Just remember to take it one step at a time," Raquel encouraged, her hand resting on his shoulder.

As they continued to discuss his plans, Ben felt the anticipation building within him. He knew he was about to embark on a journey that would not only change the lives of the boys but would also challenge him in ways he couldn't yet imagine. With Raquel by his side, he felt more determined than ever to take on this challenge, ready to become the mentor those boys so desperately needed.

Chapter III

The following morning, the sun rose bright and early, casting golden rays across the Bennett home. Ben woke up with a renewed sense of purpose, the folder of student profiles still fresh in his mind. He lay in bed for a moment, staring at the ceiling as thoughts of the boys filled his head. Today would be the first step toward making a real difference in their lives, and he felt the weight of responsibility settle on his shoulders.

"Ben, are you up?" Raquel's voice called from the kitchen, interrupting his thoughts.

"Yeah, I'm up!" he replied, swinging his legs over the side of the bed and stretching. He felt a mix of excitement and anxiety, the latter nagging at him like a persistent itch. Would the boys respond positively to his outreach? Would they trust him?

As he moved into the kitchen, he found Raquel preparing breakfast, the smell of pancakes wafting through the air. She turned to him with a smile that instantly lightened his mood.

"Morning! I made your favorite," she said, flipping a pancake onto a plate.

"Thanks, Raq. You always know how to make my day better," Ben said, taking a seat at the table. He took a moment to appreciate the warmth of home before digging into his breakfast.

After a hearty meal, Ben reviewed the profiles again, mentally preparing for the conversation he would have with each boy. He felt a surge of determination, knowing he needed to be genuine and relatable. He had to show them that he wasn't just a firefighter; he was someone who truly cared about their futures.

At around 1 PM, he decided to head to the school. He took a few moments to calm his nerves, reminding himself of Raquel's encouragement. As he drove through the familiar streets of his community, he spotted the high school looming in the distance, its brick façade standing strong against the afternoon sun.

Pulling into the school parking lot, he noticed a group of students hanging around the entrance, laughing and joking. A few were engaged in animated discussions, while others seemed disinterested, leaning against the wall, and avoiding eye contact with teachers nearby. It was a vivid reminder of the challenges the boys he would mentor faced daily.

Once inside the building, Ben made his way to Principal Harris's office. He could feel his heart pounding in his chest, but he pushed the nerves aside. This was important. He needed to focus.

"Hey, Ben!" Principal Harris greeted him warmly as he stepped into the office. "Ready for the big day?"

"Ready as I'll ever be," Ben replied, trying to match the principal's enthusiasm.

"Good to hear! I have the list of students ready for you. Are you prepared to meet them?" Principal Harris asked, gesturing for Ben to sit down.

"Absolutely," Ben said, sitting on the edge of his seat. "I've been thinking about how I want to approach our first meeting."

The principal slid a folder across the desk, and Ben took it, feeling the weight of the task ahead of him. "Here are the boys. Each of them has their own set of challenges, but I believe they can all benefit from your mentorship."

Ben opened the folder, scanning the names of the seven boys: Jeremiah, DeAndre, Xavier, Isaiah, Khalil, Andre, and Terrence. Each profile included details about their backgrounds, interests, and the struggles they faced at home and school.

"Wow, these kids have been through a lot," Ben murmured, feeling a deep sense of empathy for them. "I just hope I can reach them."

"You will," Principal Harris said confidently. "But remember, it won't happen overnight. Building trust takes time. Start by creating a safe space for them."

Ben nodded, understanding the weight of those words. "What do you suggest for the first meeting?"

"I recommend keeping it casual. Let them know who you are and why you want to help. Share your experiences, and encourage them to open up," the principal advised. "Make it a conversation rather than a lecture."

"That sounds good. I want them to feel like they can be honest with me," Ben said, his heart racing at the thought of making a connection.

"Exactly," Principal Harris replied, his eyes bright with enthusiasm. "Let's gather them in the cafeteria after school. I'll let the boys know you're coming so they'll be prepared."

Ben took a deep breath, feeling the adrenaline rush through him. "Okay, I'll see you there."

After leaving the principal's office, Ben had about an hour to prepare himself. He wandered through the halls, observing the students, trying to gauge their energy and attitudes. He saw some boys joking with friends, while others sat alone, lost in their thoughts.

As he walked past the cafeteria, he glanced inside and noticed a few of the boys he would be meeting. DeAndre was laughing with his friends, while Jeremiah sat quietly at a table, looking thoughtful. Ben's heart went out to them; he could sense the complexity behind their faces.

Finally, the bell rang, signaling the end of the school day. Ben made his way to the cafeteria, his palms sweaty and his heart racing. He pushed the door open, stepping inside the bustling room filled with chatter and laughter. The smell of pizza wafted through the air, and the sound of trays clattering mixed with the laughter of students.

"Alright, everyone, settle down!" Principal Harris called, and the room gradually quieted down. "I have a special guest today who wants to share something important with you all."

Ben took a deep breath, stepping forward as the eyes of the room shifted to him. "Hey everyone, I'm Ben Bennett, a firefighter in the community. I'm here because I want to help some of you."

He glanced around, seeing varying expressions—curiosity, skepticism, and indifference. "I've noticed some challenges that many of you are facing, and I believe that mentorship can make a difference. I want to work with you, not as a figure of authority, but as someone who can support you in navigating your lives."

The room was silent, and he could feel the tension in the air. "I know you might be thinking, 'What does this guy know about my life?' And that's fair. I'm here to listen to you, to understand what you're going through."

Jeremiah raised his hand, breaking the silence. "What's in it for you?"

Ben smiled, relieved that someone was willing to engage. "Great question. I genuinely want to see you all succeed. I've seen too many kids get caught up in a cycle that leads nowhere. I want to help you find your path, whatever that may be."

"Why should we trust you?" DeAndre chimed in, crossing his arms defiantly.

"That's a valid concern," Ben replied, feeling the weight of the moment. "Trust is built over time, and I can't expect you to trust me immediately. But I promise to be honest and transparent. If you give me a chance, I hope to earn your trust through my actions."

A murmur of conversation rippled through the room, and Ben could see the boys exchanging glances. He took a step closer to them, lowering his voice. "I've faced my own challenges. I grew up in a neighborhood similar to this one, and I've had my share of struggles. I know it's not easy, and I want to help you find a better path." The room was still, and for a moment, he felt the collective weight of their skepticism. "If you're interested, I'd love to meet with each of you one-on-one to hear your stories and understand how I can help. No pressure; it's entirely up to you."

As he concluded his speech, he felt a mix of relief and apprehension. He had laid his intentions bare, and now it was up to them to decide whether or not to engage.

Principal Harris stepped in, "Thank you, Ben. I believe this could be a valuable opportunity for all of you. Take some time to think about it, and if you're interested, let me know. We can set up some individual meetings to discuss your goals and how Ben can support you."

As the room began to buzz with chatter again, Ben stepped back, feeling a wave of uncertainty wash over him. He had opened the door, but would they walk through it?

With that thought lingering in his mind, he left the cafeteria, feeling both anxious and hopeful. He knew the journey ahead would be filled with challenges, but he was ready to take the next step. As he walked back to his truck, he couldn't shake the feeling that he had made progress today—no matter how small.

Chapter IV

The sun dipped low in the sky, casting long shadows across the parking lot as Ben drove home. His mind buzzed with thoughts of the day's events. He had shared his intentions with the boys, but now he faced the daunting challenge of waiting for their responses. Would they take a chance on him?

As he parked his truck in the driveway, Raquel stepped out onto the porch, her face lighting up when she saw him. "Hey, how did it go?" she asked, her eyes sparkling with curiosity.

"It went well, I think. I introduced myself to the boys and shared why I want to help them," Ben replied, stepping onto the porch to join her.

"That's great! What did they say?" Raquel leaned against the porch railing, eager to hear more.

"Honestly? It was a mixed bag. Some were curious, others skeptical," he admitted, rubbing the back of his neck. "I can't blame them, though. They've likely had adults make promises before that fell through."

Raquel nodded thoughtfully. "It sounds like you're off to a good start, even if it didn't go perfectly. Building trust takes time."

"Yeah, I just hope they're willing to give me a chance," Ben said, his brow furrowing with concern. "I want to make a difference, but I can't do that if they don't want to engage."

"You're a good person, Ben. They'll see that in time," Raquel reassured him. "Why don't you tell me more about the boys? Maybe we can come up with some ideas together."

As they moved inside, Ben began recounting the brief impressions he'd formed during his first meeting. He described each boy in detail—their personalities, the little quirks he noticed, and the challenges they faced.

"There's Jeremiah. He seems deep in thought all the time like he's carrying a heavy burden," Ben explained, leaning against the kitchen counter. "Then there's DeAndre, who's a bit of a class clown. He has this way of making everyone laugh, but I can sense there's more beneath the surface. He's using humor to mask something."

Raquel listened intently, encouraging him to continue. "And what about the others?" she asked.

"Xavier is a standout athlete, but I can tell he feels pressure to perform and maybe even fit in with a rough crowd," Ben added. "Khalil, on the other hand, seems a bit withdrawn. He didn't engage much today. I want to find a way to reach him."

"Sounds like you've already made some observations," Raquel noted, pouring them both a cup of coffee. "What's your plan for the next meeting?"

"I was thinking of having some group activities that promote teamwork," Ben suggested. "Something to help break the ice and encourage them to open up."

"That's a solid idea. It could help them see each other as allies rather than competitors," Raquel agreed. "What kind of activities are you considering?"

"I've been toying with the idea of doing some team-building exercises—like a small obstacle course or group challenges that require collaboration," Ben replied. "I want them to feel comfortable working together and relying on each other."

"I love that! Maybe you can even throw in some rewards for the winners," Raquel added, a smile on her face. "Kids love a little competition, and it can motivate them to engage more."

"Exactly," Ben said, feeling a spark of excitement. "I'll need to get some supplies together and plan out the details. But first, I need to see if they're interested in continuing this."

That evening, as Ben sat at the dining table with Raquel, they brainstormed ideas for engaging the boys. They discussed how to make the activities relevant to their lives and how to incorporate lessons about trust, respect, and teamwork into the mix.

Meanwhile, Ben couldn't shake the anxiety of the unknown. What if they didn't show up? What if he failed to connect with them?

As if sensing his unease, Raquel reached across the table and squeezed his hand. "You're doing everything right, Ben. Just keep being yourself, and they'll respond to your sincerity."

After dinner, Ben turned in early, feeling mentally drained but hopeful. He set his alarm for an early morning, determined to prepare thoroughly for the next day's meeting.

The following morning, the sky was overcast, a sharp contrast to the bright optimism he had felt the day before. Ben shook off the clouds of doubt and focused on the task ahead. He made a list of activities he wanted to try and gathered supplies from the local store.

Once he arrived at the school, he felt a surge of adrenaline coursing through him. He had set up cones in the gymnasium to mark out an obstacle course and arranged tables for group discussions. He could feel the energy in the air, a mixture of anticipation and nervousness.

As the students began to file in, Ben greeted them with a smile. He could see some familiar faces among the group—Jeremiah, DeAndre, and Xavier. They looked curious, their expressions reflecting the uncertainty of what was to come.

"Hey everyone, welcome back!" Ben called out, clapping his hands to grab their attention. "I'm glad to see you all again. Today, we're going to have some fun while working together as a team."

DeAndre stepped forward, a playful smirk on his face. "What's the challenge today, Mr. Bennett? Are we going to race or something?"

"Something like that! We'll be doing an obstacle course, but with a twist," Ben replied, excitement bubbling in his voice. "You'll have to work together to complete it, and I promise there'll be some prizes for the winning team."

The boys exchanged glances, and Ben could see their initial hesitation begin to fade. He could sense a flicker of interest, which spurred him on.

As they split into teams, Ben watched as they interacted with each other, the camaraderie slowly building. Jeremiah seemed to step into a leadership role, encouraging his teammates, while Xavier used his athletic skills to help navigate the course.

"Come on, we can do this!" Jeremiah shouted as they tackled the first challenge, a series of hurdles that required both strategy and communication.

Ben felt a swell of pride watching the boys work together, their laughter filling the gym as they pushed through each obstacle. The initial barriers of distrust began to crumble, replaced by shouts of encouragement and shared victories.

However, amidst the fun, Ben remained vigilant, knowing that this was only the beginning. He wanted to ensure that their progress didn't just end with games and laughter. He had to dig deeper, to help them understand that they were capable of much more than they realized.

As the activity came to a close, Ben gathered the boys together. "You all did an amazing job today! I'm proud of how you worked as a team. This is just the start of what we can accomplish together."

DeAndre grinned, a spark of mischief in his eyes. "What do we get for winning?"

Ben laughed. "How about a pizza party next week? I'll bring the pizza, and we'll celebrate your teamwork."

The boys cheered, their spirits lifted. As the meeting came to an end, Ben could feel the shift in the atmosphere. It wasn't just about the games; it was about building connections, trust, and a sense of belonging.

As they left the gym, Ben felt a surge of hope. This was only the beginning, but it felt promising. He watched as the boys headed off, exchanging jokes and laughter, the sense of camaraderie palpable in the air.

Ben returned to his truck with a smile on his face. He had taken the first step, and he was determined to keep moving forward. He couldn't wait to see where this journey would lead him and the boys he had grown to care about so much.

Chapter V

After a busy day at the station, Ben arrived at the high school cafeteria in the late afternoon, setting up for the pizza party and organizing a small area for their session afterward. It wasn't just about the food; he wanted to build trust with the boys, to show them he was invested in who they were and where they were headed.

One by one, the boys trickled in. Jeremiah was the first, taking a seat with a cautious nod in Ben's direction. The others soon followed—DeAndre, Xavier, Isaiah, Khalil, Andre, and Terrence. Their faces lit up as they spotted the pizzas, and the room quickly filled with excited chatter.

"Alright, boys, dig in!" Ben said, stepping back to let them have at it. He watched as they joked and reached for slice after slice, clearly enjoying themselves.

"Mr. Bennett, this is awesome," DeAndre said, grabbing another slice. "We don't get this kinda hookup often."

Ben smiled. "Well, you guys are putting in the work, and that deserves some recognition. Keep it up, and this won't be the last time we do something like this."

As the pizza dwindled, Ben gathered them around for a team-building activity. He handed each boy a piece of paper and a marker. "I want each of you to write down a challenge you're facing right now. Don't put your name on it— just write whatever's on your mind."

The boys exchanged glances, a little hesitant but eventually bending over their papers. When they finished, Ben collected the papers, shuffled them, and began reading them out loud.

"One of you wrote, 'I feel like I'll always be seen as trouble, even if I change,'" Ben read aloud. The room went silent. The boys avoided eye contact, but each knew that feeling.

Ben set the paper down and looked at them. "I understand. I felt the same way when I was younger. I grew up being told I was never going to make it past the streets. But you're all here because you're trying, and that's the first step to proving everyone wrong."

As he moved to the next part of the activity, he noticed some of the boys relaxing, and their guard slowly coming down. Ben set up a small assembly activity with firefighting gear, letting the boys work together to build trust and teamwork. He used this time to pull each one aside for a quick one-on-one, where he hoped to connect with them on a deeper level.

He started with Jeremiah, pulling him aside as the others continued with the activity. "Hey, I noticed you like to jump in and get things started. I bet you've got a strong voice in the group."

Jeremiah shrugged, a small smile breaking through. "Yeah, they call me 'JJ' 'cause I talk too much sometimes."

Ben laughed. "JJ, huh? I like that. Nothing wrong with having a voice—you just gotta learn how to use it to lead."

Next, he pulled aside DeAndre, who seemed a bit more reserved but had a confidence that shone through. "What about you, DeAndre? You're the quiet thinker, aren't you?"

"Yeah, but everyone calls me Dre," he replied with a smirk. "I like to stay outta trouble and just do my thing."

"Dre," Ben repeated, nodding. "You seem like the kind of guy people can rely on. I'm sure the group looks up to you, whether you know it or not."

One by one, Ben continued through the group, pulling aside each boy to hear their stories. Xavier introduced himself as 'X,' a nickname that gave him a sense of pride and mystery. Isaiah went by 'Izzy,' a nickname his little sister gave him that just stuck. Khalil, or 'Kal' as the boys called him, was tough on the outside but hinted at a softer side in his quiet moments. And then there was Terrence, who went by 'Terry.' He was the joker, always cracking a joke to lighten the mood but using humor to hide his vulnerabilities.

With each conversation, Ben felt like he was uncovering another layer. These weren't just boys with struggles—they were individuals with dreams, strengths, and potential that no one had ever taken the time to see.

As he wrapped up his last one-on-one with Terry, he returned to the group to check on the progress of their team activity. They had managed to assemble most of the equipment, albeit in a slightly chaotic fashion.

Ben clapped his hands together. "Not bad, boys! A little messy, but teamwork is about figuring it out together. And trust me, you'll get better with time."

They all chuckled, feeling a little more at ease. The names, the conversations, and the pizza party had created a warmth in the room—a sense of belonging they hadn't felt in a long time. Before they left, Ben gathered them in a circle.

"I want you all to know something. You're not here because someone's doing you a favor. You're here because each of you has something valuable to offer. Every one of you has a purpose, and my job is to help you find it."

They nodded, some with newfound respect, others with a glimmer of hope they'd long forgotten.

As Ben watched them head out, he felt a deep sense of responsibility settle over him. These boys weren't just mentees—they were young men he was determined to guide, protect, and uplift, whatever it took.

Chapter VI

A few weeks into the mentorship program, Ben began to see the boys grow more comfortable around him. Their personalities were shining through, and the group was finally starting to trust each other. Today, he decided to take them on a field trip to the fire station, hoping to give them a hands-on taste of what his world was like and to teach them some basic firefighting skills.

The boys arrived that afternoon, clearly excited but trying to play it cool. Ben noticed JJ, Dre, X, Izzy, Kal, and Terry's curiosity sparking as they stepped into the station.

"Alright, fellas," Ben said, gesturing around the station. "This is where it all happens. I know some of you think of it as just a building with a few fire trucks, but this place is a second home for us. We spend as much time here as we do at our own houses."

The boys nodded, intrigued. For some of them, having a safe place to call home was a foreign concept, and the idea of a "second home" resonated more deeply than Ben expected.

After giving them a quick tour, Ben led them to the garage where the fire trucks were parked. He started explaining each piece of equipment, from the hoses and ladders to the Jaws of Life. He could tell they were fascinated—especially X, who kept asking questions about every tool.

"Could we try lifting that?" X asked, pointing to a heavy hydraulic tool.

Ben grinned, impressed by his eagerness. "Sure thing. Come on over here, and I'll show you how to handle it. It's called the Jaws of Life. We use it to cut through metal, usually to rescue people trapped in cars after accidents."

X picked it up with Ben's guidance, struggling a bit but managing to hold the tool steady. "This thing's heavy," he admitted, his bravado dropping for a moment.

"Trust me," Ben chuckled, "it's not just heavy— it's life-saving. Every piece of equipment here has a purpose. Same as you all."

JJ, never one to miss an opportunity for a joke, chimed in, "So if I save someone, can I be the hero of the day?"

Ben laughed. "Being a hero isn't just about saving people—it's about being responsible, consistent, and committed to doing what's right, even when it's hard. You don't need a fire to prove that."

The mood shifted slightly, and he could tell they were taking his words to heart. Moving on, he led them to the firefighter uniforms hanging by the lockers. "Alright, who wants to try on the gear?"

Terry shot his hand up, unable to contain his excitement. "I'm in!"

With a grin, Ben handed him the helmet, jacket, and boots. Terry struggled a bit to put everything on, but once he was fully geared up, he struck a goofy pose, making everyone laugh. "This is heavy!" Terry exclaimed, nearly tripping over the oversized boots. "How do you guys even move in this?"

"It's all about training," Ben said. "It may feel heavy now, but when you're out there, adrenaline kicks in. You'd be surprised what you can do when someone's life depends on it."

As they continued trying on the gear and asking questions, Ben decided it was time to bring the group together for a more personal moment. He led them to a quiet corner of the station where a plaque hung on the wall, honoring a former firefighter who had lost his life in the line of duty.

"This is Marcus Phillips," Ben said quietly, pointing to the plaque. "He was one of the best firefighters I knew. Always went out of his way to help people, both on and off duty. One day, he didn't come back."

The boys fell silent, their expressions turning solemn.

Ben continued, "Being a firefighter isn't easy, and it comes with sacrifices. But Marcus believed that his life had meaning because he was doing something bigger than himself. That's what I want each of you to think about. Life is about more than just making it through the day—it's about finding something worth standing up for."

He could see the impact his words had on them. For the first time, he saw JJ's humor fade as he looked at the plaque with respect. X seemed deep in thought, processing the weight of Ben's words.

"Alright," Ben said, breaking the tension, "let's end on a lighter note. How about a quick drill?" He showed them how to handle the fire hose, and each boy took a turn trying to control the heavy stream of water. They laughed, got soaked, and cheered each other on. For a moment, they weren't just boys from difficult backgrounds—they were a team, working together, and supporting one another.

After the drill, they regrouped inside, exhausted but exhilarated. Ben handed each of them a water bottle and sat with them in a circle.

"Now, I know we had fun today, but I also want you to think about what it means to be part of something. You all have each other's backs, right?"

They nodded, some more confidently than others.

"Good," Ben said. "Because having each other's backs doesn't stop here. I expect you to look out for each other in and out of here. That's how a team works. You don't leave anyone behind."

As the boys left the station that day, Ben felt a sense of pride. He could see the spark in their eyes, the glimpse of potential. This was only the beginning, but it was a step in the right direction. He had planted a seed, one he hoped would grow into something strong and lasting.

Chapter VII

Ben was beginning to notice real progress in the boys he was working with. His training program was coming together nicely, and he could feel a noticeable shift in their attitudes. They were starting to embrace the important values of teamwork and discipline that firefighting demanded. It was clear to him that they were evolving, and he felt optimistic about their development.

On Tuesday, Ben took them to a field just outside of town to put their skills to the test. The sun was shining, and the excitement in the air was palpable. He laid out helmets, gloves, hoses, and other essential firefighting equipment on the ground. It wasn't just a set of tasks today; it was going to be a real challenge that required their focus and commitment.

Before starting, Ben took a moment to look at each boy standing before him. They had come a long way since those early days of their training, and he felt a sense of pride at how far they had progressed. However, he was aware that today's exercise would push them beyond their limits.

"All right, listen up, everyone. Today's exercise is all about trust and resilience," Ben said, his voice steady and serious. "When you're out in the field, there's no room for hesitation or mistrust. You're depending on each other's strengths, and one weak link...well, that can have serious consequences."

JJ, who was known for his confidence, smirked and replied, "I got this, Mr. Ben. This won't be nothin'." Ben raised an eyebrow and gave JJ a knowing look. "Is that so, JJ? Well, let's see if you're still saying that by the end of the day."

The playful smirk faded from JJ's face as he looked down. He understood that this exercise was more than just a simple task; it held deeper significance, and Ben's serious tone made that clear.

After that, Ben explained the specific roles for each boy. He paired them up and gave everyone a distinct task, whether it was operating the hose, carrying equipment, or setting up supports. Every job was crucial, and they would need to communicate effectively and rely on one another to succeed.

As the exercise began, Dre and JJ took charge of the hose, their expressions shifting from casual excitement to focused determination. Meanwhile, AJ and Izzy hustled to move equipment, with Kal standing on the sidelines and shouting out helpful instructions. They didn't exchange many words, but Ben could see that the boys were naturally falling into a rhythm and working together as a team.

About an hour into the exercise, Ben noticed that AJ's face was tightening in frustration as he struggled with a particularly heavy piece of equipment. He could hear AJ breathing heavily, clearly feeling the strain. "This thing's heavy, man!" AJ muttered, the fatigue evident in his voice.

"Quit whining, AJ!" Kal called out from across the field. "Just keep it moving!" Ben was about to intervene when X stepped up beside AJ and gave him a supportive pat on the shoulder. "Yo, you got this, man. Just a little more, alright?"

AJ shot X a tired but appreciative nod and adjusted his stance, his steps becoming steadier. Ben felt a surge of pride at the sight; X's encouragement had given AJ the boost he needed to keep pushing through.

Finally, after several hours of hard work, they wrapped up the exercise. The boys were clearly exhausted, their clothes soaked in sweat, but there was a sparkle of pride shining in their eyes. They gathered around Ben, eager to hear his feedback on how they performed.

Ben folded his arms across his chest, a faint smile spreading across his face. "You did well today. This is what it takes—not just in firefighting, but in life too. Sometimes it's not about being the strongest. It's about knowing when to lean on the person next to you."

Kal looked up, processing this information. "So, you're saying we gotta have each other's backs...like, no matter what?"

Ben met Kal's gaze directly. "Exactly. Out there in the field, you can't second-guess each other. You don't have that option. Trust is what keeps you safe and gets you home."

JJ, his usual confidence somewhat subdued, glanced around at the others before returning his focus to Ben. "Guess I didn't think about it like that. I mean, really having to trust someone, you know?"

Ben nodded, giving JJ's shoulder a reassuring squeeze. "You're all learning, and that's what matters. Trust isn't built overnight. But if you keep this up, you'll surprise yourselves with what you can achieve."

As they began to pack up the gear, Ben felt a wave of hope wash over him. The boys were changing, proving not only to him but also to themselves that they were capable of so much more than anyone had ever believed. They were on a path of growth, and he was excited to see where it would lead them.

Chapter VIII

Winter was creeping in, and with it, a biting chill in the air, but Ben's weekly sessions were only getting more intense. The boys were settling into the mentorship program's rhythm, but Ben knew they needed a crucial lesson on resilience—a test of character and strength under pressure.

That week, Ben brought them to an abandoned, burned-down building on the outskirts of town, used occasionally for fire department training. The building, darkened by char and dusted with ash, held a lingering smell of smoke, reminding them all of the power of destruction.

"Alright, guys," Ben began, gathering the group outside, "today we're doing a live scenario. This exercise is going to test how you handle fear, pressure, and setbacks. This isn't about perfection; it's about sticking together and thinking on your feet."

The boys looked at each other, nerves evident in their eyes. Terry shot Ben a steady look, though he fidgeted with his helmet. Dre's gaze was glued to the ground, while JJ scanned the ominous building in front of them.

"What if we mess up, Mr. Ben?" Terry asked, his usually calm voice edged with unease.

"You will mess up," Ben replied, meeting each of their eyes. "But you've got each other. Stick together, trust your instincts, and learn from whatever happens."

Ben handed them helmets and flashlights, walking them through their roles. The goal was to find and "rescue" a mannequin somewhere inside, representing a missing person. Each boy would have a job, but success meant working as a team.

As they stepped into the building, the darkness and stale smoke intensified their anxiety. Kal led, taking cautious steps, his flashlight beam cutting through the shadows. Dre and AJ moved in behind him, while Terry, JJ, and X covered the rear.

"Stay close," Kal whispered, trying to hide the tremor in his voice. "And watch out for anything loose."

They crept forward, each boy's breathing audible over the silence. A loud crash startled them as a chunk of debris fell. JJ jumped, and his helmet knocked against the wall.

"Yo, chill, JJ," X muttered, though his own voice shook.

"Everyone good?" Kal asked, his eyes darting over them.

They nodded, regaining their composure. Ben watched from a safe distance, proud of how they handled the first scare.

They were making good progress until Dre tripped on a broken beam, letting out a pained grunt as he fell to his knees.

"Ah, man, this isn't good," Dre mumbled, rubbing his knee, trying to brush off the pain.

The others stopped, looking back at him. Terry, without hesitation, knelt beside Dre. "You're not sitting this out. Lean on me if you need to. We're getting through this."

AJ and JJ moved closer, positioning themselves to offer support, while Kal checked their surroundings. "Let's go slow," he said, reassuring Dre. "We've got your back."

With Dre supported on either side, they continued inching forward. Their steps were slower but steadier. Despite the tension, Ben could see the bond strengthening with each move and whispered exchange. It was no longer about passing a test but about carrying each other through the challenge.

After what felt like hours in the dark, Terry's flashlight caught the mannequin in the corner of a small, charred room. "Found it!" he called, excitement breaking through his exhaustion.

The group shuffled forward, lifting the mannequin together, their movements synchronized by the unspoken determination that had grown between them. They emerged from the building, faces smeared with ash, helmets askew, but each boy's eyes gleamed with pride.

Ben approached, nodding as he surveyed the group. "You all did incredible. That was tough, but none of you left Dre behind. None of you let the fear stop you."

Terry looked back at the others, a rare smile breaking across his face. "Guess we didn't really have a choice, huh? We had to stick together."

Ben grinned, resting a hand on Terry's shoulder. "That's exactly the point. You're stronger as a team. When life throws real challenges your way, remember this. You've proven you can lean on each other."

The boys exchanged nods, each one feeling the weight of what they'd just accomplished. In their own way, they'd become a unit—a family bound by trust and loyalty. Ben knew that whatever life threw at them next, they were ready to face it together.

Chapter IX

The usual chatter died down as the boys filed into the small room at the fire station, a space Ben had set up for their weekly sessions. This wasn't a typical training day. Today, he wanted them to talk—to give them a space to unpack the weight they carried every day. For the first time, all seven boys—JJ, Dre, Izzy, X, Kal, AJ, and Terry—were together, sitting around in a rough circle, each carrying their own guarded expression.

Ben cleared his throat, breaking the silence. "Today, I don't want us to just talk about firefighting or drills. I want us to open up about what's on our minds, the things that might be weighing us down." He looked at each of them, hoping to catch a glimmer of trust. "This is a safe space. Anything shared here stays here."

A tense quiet filled the room. For a moment, he wasn't sure if anyone would be willing to speak up. But after a few moments, JJ leaned forward, glancing around before he spoke.

"It's… It's tough out there, man. My dad's been gone a while, and my mom works all the time. Feels like I'm the man of the house, but half the time, I don't even know what that means." He shrugged, his shoulders heavy. "I just feel like I'm always guessing at what to do, and sometimes, it's like… I can't get it right, no matter how hard I try."

Ben nodded, giving JJ a reassuring look. "That's a lot of weight to carry, JJ. It's okay to feel unsure. You're doing the best you can, and that's more than enough."

JJ's admission seemed to open a door. Next, Dre spoke up, his voice steady but laced with frustration. "My uncle's in and out of trouble, and everyone at home expects me to be just like him. I don't want to be, but they don't believe I'll ever be anything different." He clenched his fists. "Feels like no one sees me for me. Just another kid from the neighborhood, right?"

"Dre, you're already proving them wrong by showing up here," Ben said. "You don't have to be anyone but yourself. You have a choice, and you're making it every time you decide to come here instead of following what's expected."

Izzy, who often stayed quiet in these sessions, took a deep breath and began to speak. "I'm just tired of always being overlooked. I don't feel like I matter to anybody." His voice trailed off, and he looked down, unable to meet anyone's gaze. "Sometimes, I think maybe it'd be better if I wasn't here at all."

A heavy silence followed his words, each boy feeling the weight of Izzy's honesty. Ben reached out a hand, steady and compassionate. "Izzy, you do matter. We see you. You're part of this group, and we're here for you."

X broke in, his voice rough. "I get what he means. People look at me and see my record, and that's all they care about. I'm more than that, but nobody bothers to look deeper. Like, yeah, I've made mistakes, but I'm trying to change. Isn't that worth something?"

"It's worth everything," Ben replied, looking at X. "You don't have to be defined by the past. You're showing up, putting in the work, and that says a lot about who you are."

Kal, usually the joker of the group, surprised everyone by speaking up next. "For me, it's all about proving people wrong. My brothers never made it out of our situation, and I don't want to end up the same way. But it's hard when you feel like you're expected to fail."

"Expectations don't define you, Kal. Your actions do," Ben encouraged. "Every choice you make is shaping who you are, not what others expect you to be."

Terry, quiet but observant, finally added his own story. "My family... they're not really around. Foster homes, bounce from place to place. Makes it hard to trust anyone, you know?" He looked at the floor, his voice barely above a whisper. "Every time I think things are getting better, I get moved again. It's like I'm just waiting for people to leave."

The room felt heavier with each confession, the vulnerability creating a powerful, shared silence. Ben felt the pain in each boy's story, a weight pressing down on him, but also a quiet resolve to lift them out of it. "Terry, trust takes time, especially when life's been unpredictable. But I want you to know that I'm here. I'm not going anywhere."

AJ was the last to speak. He looked around, hesitant, but then he let out a sigh. "My cousin, he got into some serious trouble a while back. And it's like every adult in my life thinks I'm gonna end up like him. Sometimes I wonder if they're right... like maybe it's just in my blood or something."

Ben shook his head firmly. "AJ, your path is yours alone. We can be influenced by family, but we get to decide our own futures. And the fact that you're here, fighting for a different path, proves that you're already making a different choice."

The boys nodded slowly, absorbing Ben's words. It was clear this was the first time many of them had ever shared these fears and burdens aloud. They looked at each other, something unspoken passing between them. They were a group now, bonded not just by the firehouse but by their shared struggles.

After a moment, Ben continued, leaning forward and looking each of them in the eye. "I know life hasn't been easy for any of you. You've all been through things that no kid should have to face. But I want you to understand something: you're not alone anymore. We're a team. We've got each other's backs, and we're going to get through this together."

JJ, who had started the conversation, looked around at his friends, and then back at Ben. "I didn't think I'd be able to talk about this stuff, but... it actually feels better. Like maybe I don't have to carry it all on my own."

Dre nodded in agreement. "Yeah. Same here. I didn't think any of y'all would understand. But we're all in this mess together, huh?"

Each of the boys echoed their agreement, a quiet strength building between them. They realized that while their struggles were unique, the pain and uncertainty were something they all shared. There was comfort in that, a rare sense of understanding they hadn't experienced before.

Ben leaned back, letting the silence settle. He knew the power of this moment, that these boys needed this trust, this connection, as much as they needed the guidance he was trying to offer. "This journey won't be easy, and there are still going to be tough days. But you have the strength to get through it. I believe in each and every one of you."

He paused, his gaze steady. "And I want each of you to take something away from today. You don't have to do this alone. Lean on each other. Lean on me. We're stronger together."

The boys looked around the circle, their expressions shifting from guarded to something close to hopeful. JJ cracked a small smile, and Dre gave a nod of approval. They were far from perfect, far from fully trusting, but they were taking the first steps.

The session wrapped up, but no one rushed to leave. They lingered, talking quietly among themselves, sharing stories and laughs, their defenses lowered just a bit. For the first time, they were truly starting to feel like a team, a family that understood them in a way no one else could.

Ben watched them, a sense of pride swelling within him. He knew the road ahead was still long and fraught with challenges, but today was a step in the right direction. And he was willing to walk with them every step of the way.

Chapter X

In the weeks following that breakthrough session, Ben noticed a renewed commitment in each of the boys. The walls they'd built up started to crack, little by little. They didn't all have perfect attendance, and sometimes one or two of them would still come in late. But Ben saw the shift—they were putting in effort, connecting, growing. However, the journey was far from smooth, and setbacks became part of the learning curve.

One late afternoon, the group gathered in the firehouse training room. Ben had planned an intense day of drills to keep them focused, but he also knew the importance of reminding them why they were here—why they were working to build a different future. The drills helped create a rhythm, something reliable they could focus on, but today, he wanted to delve deeper.

"Alright, let's take a break," Ben announced after the last drill, catching his breath along with the boys. They slumped against the walls, sweat beading on their foreheads, but there was a steady look of determination in their eyes.

He took a seat on a bench facing them. "We've been at this for a while now, and I want to hear from you. What do you see for yourselves, once you leave here? Where do you want to go, what do you want to do?"

The boys exchanged uncertain glances, shifting under the weight of the question. It was the kind of question that felt almost too big to answer like it was a future they hadn't allowed themselves to imagine.

"JJ?" Ben prodded gently.

JJ hesitated, then looked at the floor. "I dunno… I mean, I guess I've always thought about being a mechanic or something. My cousin's got a shop, and I used to help him out. Fixing cars… it's one of the only things that ever made sense to me, you know?"

Ben smiled, giving him an encouraging nod. "That's a great goal, JJ. You're good with your hands; I can see you doing that. What about you, Izzy?"

Izzy ran a hand over his head, avoiding Ben's gaze. "Honestly, I don't know. Sometimes I think maybe I'd want to work in a gym, you know? Like, help other kids learn how to take care of themselves, keep them off the streets." He shrugged, clearly embarrassed. "It probably sounds dumb."

Ben shook his head. "That's not dumb at all. That's real. You're talking about giving back, about helping other kids avoid the struggles you've been through. That's powerful, Izzy."

Dre spoke up next, almost interrupting. "I've always liked cooking. Used to mess around in the kitchen with my grandma when I was little. She used to say I had a knack for it." He scratched the back of his neck. "Maybe I'd try working in a restaurant or something."

"A chef in the making," Ben grinned, raising an eyebrow. "Dre, I'd be first in line to eat at your restaurant."

The boys chuckled, and the mood lightened a bit. As each of them took turns sharing their aspirations, Ben noticed the way they opened up, a flicker of hope in each face. They hadn't allowed themselves to dream in a long time, and the idea of having a real future felt foreign but exciting.

Ben looked over to AJ, who had been uncharacteristically quiet. "What about you, AJ?"

AJ took a deep breath and looked at the ceiling. "Honestly, I don't know. I haven't really thought about anything after this." His voice grew softer. "Sometimes it feels like I'll always be stuck where I am. Like no matter how hard I try, I can't leave it behind."

Ben's gaze softened. "You're here, AJ. Every day, you're showing up. That's already a step forward. It's normal to feel that way but remember, you're the one who gets to decide where you're going."

AJ's face softened just a bit, and he gave Ben a brief nod.

Terry shifted uncomfortably but finally spoke up. "I thought about being a firefighter... like you, Ben. Seems like I'd have to work a lot harder to get there, but I think it'd be worth it. I like the idea of helping people, of doing something that matters."

Ben's chest swelled with pride. "Terry, if that's what you want, then it's yours to work for. And I'm here to help you every step of the way."

They continued talking, sharing snippets of who they wanted to be, dreams that had once seemed out of reach but now felt just a bit more possible. Ben knew that these conversations were crucial, giving the boys a sense of purpose they could hold onto, something to drive them on the harder days.

As they wrapped up, he glanced around, feeling a deep sense of gratitude for these moments. But he also knew setbacks were lurking, challenges that could easily unravel their progress.

A few days later, that reality hit hard. JJ missed two days in a row, and when he finally returned, his usual bright spirit was dimmed. Ben pulled him aside after the session.

"Everything okay, JJ?"

JJ's gaze darted away, and he swallowed. "Got into it with my mom's boyfriend. He thinks I'm wasting my time here, says I should be out making money instead of playing around with y'all."

Ben's heart sank. He knew how delicate JJ's home situation was, and how easily he could get pulled back into old habits. "You're not wasting time, JJ. You're building a future here. But I know it's hard when people around you don't see it that way."

JJ gave a weak nod. "Yeah. I just... I dunno. It's tough, you know?"

Ben clapped a reassuring hand on his shoulder. "You're not alone in this. And if you ever need a place to cool off, you come here. This place is yours too."

The support Ben offered wasn't lost on the other boys. They rallied around JJ, sensing that he was at a tipping point. It reminded them all how fragile their progress was, how quickly they could get pulled back into the streets if they didn't stay focused and rely on each other. At the end of the week, Dre didn't show up, and neither did AJ. This time, Ben felt the creeping frustration and worry. He knew this was part of the journey, but it hurt to see the boys stumble. The group was silent that afternoon, feeling the absence of their friends. Ben finally broke the silence, addressing their mutual disappointment. "Look, I know it's hard when not everyone's here. But remember, we can't control what other people do. All we can do is show up and be here for each other."

Terry nodded, the words hitting close. "Yeah, but... it's hard seeing everyone drop off like that. Makes it feel like we're fighting a losing battle sometimes."

Ben took a deep breath. "It's not a losing battle, Terry. We just have to keep showing up and keep fighting. Even if it's tough, even if not everyone makes it. You're each stronger than you know."

That quiet resolve seemed to settle into the boys, grounding them. They understood that setbacks were a part of their story, but so was resilience. And they knew Ben would be there, every step of the way, helping them stay on course—even when the world seemed determined to pull them back.

Chapter XI

Ben had prepared a team-building exercise for today that he hoped would deepen the boys' sense of camaraderie. He knew the boys were beginning to bond, but he wanted to foster a sense of trust and accountability that ran even deeper. He called today's drill the "Obstacle Trust Challenge," where each boy would have to rely entirely on the directions of his teammates to navigate a challenging course blindfolded. His goal was to teach them that just like in life, sometimes you had to lean on others to find your way forward.

As the boys gathered around, Ben explained the rules. "Alright, today, each of you will be blindfolded while your teammates guide you through a course. There are cones, ropes, and barriers. Your goal is to listen closely to each other, follow instructions, and make it through without touching anything. This is about trust and communication—two things you'll need more than ever as you move forward."

The boys exchanged excited and uncertain glances, and JJ was the first to raise his hand. "I'll go first, I guess."

Ben handed JJ a blindfold, and once it was tied, he positioned him at the start of the course. The rest of the group spread out along the path, ready to direct him.

"Take two small steps forward, but watch out for the cone on your right," Isaiah called out, his voice steady.

JJ carefully took a step forward, moving slowly, his hands slightly raised in front of him. The boys guided him around each obstacle, with a few laughs and corrections along the way. By the time he reached the end of the course, they erupted into a round of cheers and playful shoves.

"Nice work, JJ!" Khalil, or "Kal," said with a grin. He was next to volunteer, and soon the boys were guiding him with the same mix of caution and encouragement.

One by one, each boy took a turn blindfolded, working their way through the course with varying levels of confidence. When it was Dre's turn, he seemed more hesitant, pausing often and fumbling slightly.

"Dre, take it easy," X said, using his steady voice to reassure him. "We got you, just one step at a time."

Dre let out a deep breath and took another careful step, relaxing slightly as he began to trust his teammates' guidance. By the time they'd all completed the challenge, there was an easy laughter and a sense of accomplishment among them, as though a weight had been lifted.

"Alright, fellas," Ben said, calling them in. "Did you notice how much easier it was to trust each other the more you communicated?" The boys nodded, a few of them nudging each other playfully.

Ben motioned them toward a shaded spot nearby where they could debrief and talk. As they settled down, Ben shifted the conversation, wanting to dig a little deeper. "Today, I want to hear more about what each of you is dealing with outside of here," he said. "What obstacles are you facing right now? Let's talk about what's been hard, and maybe together, we can figure out some ways to move forward."

For a moment, the boys looked at each other, some of them fidgeting as they debated whether or not to speak up. JJ was the first to break the silence.

"Honestly," he began, looking down at his hands, "I'm still getting pulled back to my old crew. They keep hitting me up, saying all I need to do is one quick job, and I could make more than I would in a month. It's hard to say no."

The others nodded, some of them sharing knowing glances. JJ's struggle wasn't new to any of them.

Dre spoke up next, his usual confidence somewhat dimmed. "I feel that, man. For me, school has just been... hard. I've been skipping more than I should, and now I'm so far behind I don't even see the point of going. Feels like I'm just digging myself deeper."

Isaiah leaned forward, giving Dre a nod. "Same here, Dre. But if you want, I could help. I'm alright in math, so I could show you some stuff if you want to catch up."

Dre managed a small smile. "Thanks, Isaiah. I might take you up on that."

X, usually the calm and collected one, spoke up next. "Grades are rough for me, too. I don't want to fail, but sometimes it feels like no matter what I do, it's not enough. I've thought about just quitting."

The group fell silent, each boy's words carrying the weight of shared experiences. Kal, who rarely spoke about his struggles, cleared his throat.

"For me, it's family stuff. My dad's never around, and my mom's got her hands full, so there's not much help for me when it comes to school. Sometimes I feel like I'm just... alone."

Ben took in each of their stories, feeling a mix of pride and compassion. "I hear all of you, and I know it's hard," he said, his voice steady and reassuring. "But remember, you're not alone anymore. Lean on each other, lean on me. Just like in that course out there, we've got to trust one another."

As they sat in thoughtful silence, AJ spoke up, surprising everyone. "I got something, too," he said quietly. "Some days, it feels easier to just stay home. My brother's into some stuff I don't want to be around, but it's hard to leave that world behind when it's all I've ever known. Coming here helps, but it's still a battle every day."

Ben reached out, patting AJ on the shoulder. "That's real, AJ. And you're showing strength by choosing to be here, even when it's hard."

Then, in a voice barely above a whisper, Terry finally spoke. "Sometimes, I get tired of fighting the same battles. But, like... I don't know. Seeing all of you here makes it easier. I don't feel as stuck."

His words lingered in the air, the impact of their honesty palpable. The boys exchanged glances, their expressions a blend of vulnerability and newfound understanding.

Ben let the silence stretch, wanting them to sit with the weight of what they'd shared. Then he smiled, the warmth in his gaze steady. "You're all carrying a lot, but you're not carrying it alone. You've got each other, and you've got me. Remember, if you need a hand, don't hesitate to reach out. We're a team now."

With that, he brought them in for a final cheer, the echo of their voices stronger than ever, each one holding the unspoken promise that they'd face whatever came next—together.

Chapter XII

Ben gathered the boys at the fire station early that Saturday morning. The atmosphere was charged with anticipation as they geared up, strapping on helmets and securing gloves. Today's practical was set to test not only their endurance but also their trust in one another.

"Alright, listen up," Ben said, his voice commanding but encouraging. "Today, we're running a simulated rescue. This drill is all about teamwork and communication. You'll each have specific roles, and it's up to you to make this work. No one is left behind. Got it?"

The boys nodded, excitement mixed with a bit of nervousness in their faces.

They split into teams, with Ben assigning each boy a responsibility. JJ and X would handle the search inside the simulated "burning" structure. Dre and Isaiah were tasked with guiding them from the outside using only radios, keeping track of their teammates' movements through the maze of dark, smoke-filled rooms. Kal and Terry were assigned to handle the equipment, while AJ was responsible for keeping everyone hydrated and keeping track of time.

Once everyone was in position, Ben turned to JJ and X. "You two, remember, don't just rush in. Communicate. Keep each other safe."

JJ smirked at X, his competitive spirit flaring. "Let's do this, man. Got your back."

X nodded, a rare smile crossing his usually stoic face. "Same."

With a sharp whistle, Ben signaled the start. JJ and X moved quickly but carefully, talking into their radios as they went, relying on Dre and Isaiah's guidance. Outside, Dre's voice crackled over the radio, giving directions with precise calm, even as he struggled with his nerves. Isaiah was watching Dre's directions, adding his own feedback whenever he noticed JJ and X going off course.

The first few minutes went smoothly, but as they delved deeper into the exercise, frustrations began bubbling up. X couldn't locate the dummy they were supposed to "rescue," and he started snapping into the radio. "Dre, where am I? It's pitch-black in here!"

Dre took a shaky breath. "You're close, man. Take two steps forward... then right."

JJ interrupted, "Man, we're wasting time. Let's just try another room."

Isaiah chimed in, trying to ease the tension, "Guys, Dre's doing his best. Stick with it."

Outside, Kal and Terry were struggling with the heavy equipment. Kal huffed, "This is harder than it looks. Ain't no way I thought hauling hoses could be this rough."

Terry grinned at him, sweating but determined. "Better this than the streets, right?"

As the exercise continued, each team felt the strain of their roles. AJ jogged between everyone, handing out water and offering words of encouragement, while Ben kept a watchful eye. He could see the frustrations but also the determination, and he felt a surge of pride watching them all work together.

Finally, JJ and X located the dummy, and with Dre and Isaiah's guidance, they managed to carry it out to safety. When they emerged, the boys were all panting, dripping with sweat but grinning. They'd made it.

"Good job, fellas," Ben said, clapping his hands. "Not perfect, but a solid effort. Now, let's gather round and talk."

The boys settled on benches, exhausted but satisfied. Ben looked at each one in turn.

"Today, you had to rely on each other, even when things got tough. In a real situation, that trust is everything. But I know it's not easy – not in here, and not out there." He gestured outside, where the noise of traffic and city life buzzed in the distance.

JJ shifted, his face serious. "Ben, it's harder out there. In here, we got you watching our backs. But at school... it's just us."

X added, "Yeah, man. I got teachers looking at me like I'm up to no good, even when I'm just trying to do my work."

Isaiah nodded in agreement. "Same. And when I'm actually struggling in class, they don't even notice. They just think I'm being lazy."

Ben leaned forward, meeting their gazes. "So what do we do about it? How do we face these challenges head-on?"

Kal sighed, "I'm barely passing math, man. And when I think about asking for help, it's like... who's gonna care enough to help me? Half the time, I don't even get the point of the assignments."

Isaiah's face softened as he looked over at Kal. "I'm good at math. I could help you if you want."

Kal looked surprised, a faint grin creeping onto his face. "For real?"

Isaiah nodded. "Yeah. I mean, we're all in this together, right?"

The group nodded in silent agreement. Terry cleared his throat, glancing at the ground. "Honestly, sometimes I feel like I'm the only one who gets this close to changing, but it's like the old life keeps calling me back. I walk through my neighborhood, and it's hard not to go back to old habits."

Dre spoke up, his voice quiet. "Me too, man. Got old friends I still see… they're doing the same stuff I was trying to get away from. Sometimes I miss it, but then I think about how far I've come."

AJ looked over at Ben, a question in his eyes. "Ben, how'd you stay on track? You ever feel like giving up?"

Ben looked around at the boys, his expression thoughtful. "I felt like giving up plenty of times. But I realized that change wasn't just about me. People were depending on me – my family, my community. Just like you guys have people depending on you, even if you don't realize it yet. And now, you have each other."

The boys sat in silence, each of them thinking about their own lives, the people they wanted to make proud, and the futures they dreamed of.

Ben continued, "This isn't just about firefighting. This is about who you're becoming. Every time you choose to show up here, every time you choose to put in the work, you're building a future. And you don't have to do it alone. You've got each other – and you've got me."

They all looked around, meeting each other's eyes. For the first time, there was a quiet but unspoken bond forming between them – a sense of shared purpose, of brotherhood.

"Alright, enough of the heavy stuff," Ben said, a small grin forming. "But next time, maybe don't make X carry the dummy on his own."

The boys laughed, the tension breaking, and they walked out of the fire station feeling a little lighter, their bonds a little stronger.

Chapter XIII

The following week, Ben decided to up the challenge for the boys. The practicals had been going well, but he knew they needed more than just physical exercises. They needed moments that would test their character and resilience—moments that would echo the choices they'd face in real life.

He arranged for a day at the community center, where they would meet local community members and volunteers. Ben wanted the boys to learn the importance of serving others, even when it wasn't easy or immediately rewarding. When the boys arrived, they found Ben waiting with several large boxes filled with supplies.

"Alright, fellas," Ben began, gesturing to the boxes. "Today, you're not just here to work on firefighting skills. You're here to give back. Inside these boxes are supplies for families in need—groceries, toiletries, and blankets. Our job is to organize everything into care packages and deliver them to those who need a hand."

JJ raised an eyebrow. "So we're playing delivery boys today?"

Ben gave him a steady look. "Not delivery boys, JJ. We're learning what it means to be part of a community and to serve. Not every day's about lifting weights and saving lives. Sometimes, it's the little things that make the biggest difference."

The boys began sorting the supplies, some hesitantly and others with a quiet sense of purpose. It didn't take long for the grumbling to quiet down as they fell into a rhythm, organizing packages and preparing to load them into Ben's truck for delivery.

While they worked, Ben pulled each boy aside individually to check in, using the time to dig a little deeper.

Ben started with Isaiah, who had been especially quiet that day.

"How's everything going, Isaiah? Last time, you mentioned that it's tough to stay motivated with school," Ben asked.

Isaiah shrugged, fiddling with a can of soup. "It's still hard. I know I should care, but sometimes I feel like I'm just going through the motions. It's like, even when I try, it doesn't make a difference."

Ben nodded, understanding. "Sometimes, the effort doesn't feel worth it right away. But that doesn't mean it won't be. You have more to give than you realize, Isaiah. Sometimes, you just have to keep going, even when it's hard."

Isaiah met Ben's eyes, a flicker of hope in his gaze. "Yeah, maybe you're right."

Next, he found AJ, who was carrying a large box to the truck.

"Hey, AJ, got a second?" Ben asked, stepping in to help him with the box.

AJ set it down, breathing heavily. "Sure, what's up?"

"I've noticed you're always looking out for the others. You make sure everyone's okay, check in... How're you holding up?" Ben asked.

AJ smiled sheepishly. "I just... I don't know. I guess I feel like if I don't, who will? I can't stand seeing people struggle alone."

Ben placed a hand on AJ's shoulder. "You're a natural leader, AJ. But don't forget to lean on others, too. You don't have to carry everything by yourself."

AJ nodded, a little embarrassed but grateful for the words.

He moved over to Dre, who was stacking boxes a bit rougher than usual.

"Hey, everything okay?" Ben asked.

Dre sighed, glancing away. "Just had a rough week. People in my life keep trying to pull me back to the old stuff. It's hard to say no all the time, you know?"

Ben nodded, his expression serious. "It is hard. But every time you say no, you're saying yes to something better. You're building a new path, and every step matters."

Dre took a deep breath. "I'm trying, Ben. I just hope it's worth it."

"It is, Dre. I promise," Ben assured him.

One by one, Ben had similar conversations with the rest of the boys. He learned that Kal was struggling with a family member in trouble, that Terry was dealing with pressure from friends to skip school, and that JJ had been caught in a fight defending his younger brother from a neighborhood bully.

When Ben finally gathered the boys together again, he saw something different in their expressions. Each of them had shared a part of themselves they'd been carrying alone, and the weight had lifted, even if only a little.

"All right, team," Ben said, his voice warm. "You all have battles you're fighting, and I know it's not easy. But you're not alone in this. We've got each other, and that's what matters."

The boys nodded, a quiet sense of unity forming among them. They loaded up the truck with the last of the packages and set off to make their deliveries, each of them feeling a little lighter, a little more hopeful.

As they knocked on doors and handed out supplies to grateful families, the boys started to understand the value of small acts of kindness. They saw the relief in people's eyes, the gratitude in their voices, and they realized that they had the power to make a difference—even when it wasn't in a fire station or a flashy rescue.

When they finished, Ben gathered them in a circle outside the community center.

"Today wasn't about firefighting," he said, "but it was about saving lives differently. I hope you all remember this feeling. This is what it means to be a part of something bigger than yourselves."

The boys nodded, each of them reflecting on what they'd learned. They realized that they didn't need uniforms or hoses to make an impact—they just needed the courage to show up and give what they could.

And in that moment, they took another step forward, not only as a team but as young men growing into the leaders they were becoming.

Chapter XIV

The fire station training lot buzzed with the usual chatter of the boys as they finished another round of drills. The sun hung low, casting an amber glow that hinted at the approaching evening. They were sweaty and tired, but feeling accomplished. Ben watched them closely, noting the different expressions on their faces. Some seemed lighter, carrying a quiet confidence, while others had a distant look as if weighed down by something they couldn't shake.

"All right, team," Ben called out, gathering everyone in a circle. "Let's wrap up with a check-in. I want to hear how things are going outside of here. What's working? What's not?"

The group settled in, a mix of excitement and hesitation in their faces. They had grown used to these check-ins, but tonight, Ben sensed a deeper readiness to talk.

Isaiah, "Izzy," spoke up first, a small smile on his face. "So, I helped JJ with his math test last week," he started, nudging JJ. "And guess what? My guy got a B!"

The boys erupted in cheers, clapping and playfully slapping JJ on the back. JJ grinned, clearly proud but also a little bashful.

"Yeah, man, I thought I was gonna bomb it," JJ admitted. "But Izzy broke it down for me. Stuff that used to look like gibberish started making sense."

Izzy nodded, happy to see his friend's success. "You got this, JJ. You're smarter than you think—you just needed someone to show you the steps."

Ben watched with a smile, pleased to see the boys supporting each other. But he also noticed some quieter faces among them, especially X, whose eyes were fixed on the ground.

"X," Ben prompted gently. "How about you? What's been going on?"

Xavier took a moment, his voice barely above a whisper. "It's...been tough," he admitted. "I thought things would get better after I started coming here, but my mom's still working two jobs, and I'm barely passing most of my classes. Math's just one of the things I can't seem to keep up with."

The group fell silent. They respected X's quiet determination, but they could see the frustration in his eyes.

Izzy glanced over, offering, "Hey, X, we could study together, man. I know it sounds cheesy, but it's been helping JJ. We could give it a shot."

X managed a small nod, though his expression was still uncertain. "Thanks, Izzy. I'd appreciate that."

Ben looked around the circle, his voice steady. "This is what it's all about, fellas. Not just pushing through these drills but building each other up. You each have strengths to offer, and it's okay to lean on each other when things get hard."

DeAndre, or "Dre," cleared his throat, shifting uncomfortably. "I'm trying to stay out of trouble, but some of my old friends don't get it. They keep texting me, saying I've changed, that I think I'm better than them." He looked around at the group. "It's hard to ignore them when they're right there, waiting for me outside school."

Xavier nodded, clearly understanding. "Same here, Dre. Some guys don't want to see you move forward. They'd rather pull you back."

Terry, usually one of the more reserved members of the group, suddenly spoke up, his voice firm. "You know what, though? We're all here because we want more than that. If they're trying to pull you down, then maybe they're not your friends."

Dre looked over, surprised but thoughtful. "You're right, man. I don't want to go back to that, and I know being here is better. It's just...hard sometimes."

Ben nodded, sensing the struggle in Dre's voice. "It's about taking each day as it comes, Dre. And remember, you've got a team right here who gets what you're going through."

Khalil, "Kal," who'd been mostly quiet, chimed in. "The hardest part is just getting people to see you differently. I got my history grade up last week, and my teacher actually told me she was proud of me. First time I ever heard that. But still, when I walk into school, people just see me as the kid who's always messing around."

JJ reached over and gave Kal a reassuring nudge. "People will come around, man. It just takes time. And you got us to keep you on track."

The group nodded, the support flowing among them. Ben felt a quiet satisfaction, seeing how far they'd come in opening up to one another.

"There's a lot of work ahead," Ben said, his voice steady but encouraging. "But today, you showed what this team's about. Each of you brings something unique, and you're stronger together. So let's keep building, and keep pushing forward. You've already proven you've got it in you."

The boys nodded, a renewed determination in their eyes. They still had struggles to face, but now, they had each other and a growing belief that maybe, just maybe, and they could leave their pasts behind.

Chapter XV

The group was back at the fire station, ready for another hands-on session. Today's exercise was one of the toughest yet: a search-and-rescue drill in full gear. Ben had set up a simulated "smoke-filled" room in one of the training facilities, where the boys would have to navigate blindfolded, relying only on their senses and each other to locate a "victim."

"All right, team," Ben began, adjusting his helmet. "This is about more than finding someone in the dark. You've got to communicate, trust your teammates, and stay calm under pressure. In real life, lives depend on it."

The boys geared up, adrenaline buzzing through the air. For a moment, they looked like real firefighters, each wearing a uniform that was slightly oversized but made them feel powerful.

"Let's go, squad," JJ said with a grin, his confidence lighting up the room. But as they stepped into the darkened, smoke-mimicking chamber, the seriousness of the task set in.

"Stay low, follow my voice," Terry called out, taking the lead with a sense of calmness that surprised even himself. His confidence had grown over the weeks, and he'd discovered that leading came naturally to him.

They navigated through the room, calling out to each other, hands reaching out in the thick "smoke." Every once in a while, they'd stumble or bump into a wall, but each time, someone would offer a hand, a laugh, or a quick "Keep going, we got this."

About halfway through, Dre accidentally tripped and fell to his knees, his breathing heavy as he struggled to find his footing. In the past, he might've tried to brush it off or play it cool, but now he was comfortable enough to accept the hand JJ offered him.

"Thanks, man," Dre muttered, pulling himself up, grateful for the team's support.

After nearly an hour, they made it out, "victim" in tow. Ben was waiting with a proud smile, clapping them on the back as they took off their gear and caught their breath.

"You all did amazing," Ben said, his voice full of pride. "You stayed calm, worked as a team, and didn't give up. Those are the skills that'll take you far, not just here but in life."

The boys shared proud glances, feeling the weight of Ben's words.

After a quick break, they gathered around in the lounge area, their faces still flushed from the intense training. Ben could sense that they were ready for a deeper conversation, a check-in on how things were going beyond the drills and exercises.

"So," Ben began, leaning forward. "Let's talk about what's been on your minds lately. Outside of here, what's your biggest struggle right now?"

They exchanged glances before X spoke up, his voice steady but tinged with frustration. "For me, it's staying on track with school. My grades are okay, but sometimes I just feel like giving up, you know? Like...what's the point? No one expects anything from me."

Kal nodded, chiming in. "Same here. I've been doing better in some classes, but people just see me as the kid who messed up too many times. It's like they don't believe I can actually change."

Izzy jumped in, trying to be the voice of encouragement. "You guys have been doing great. I mean, X, you've been staying after school for tutoring, right? And Kal, didn't your history teacher give you a shoutout last week?"

X cracked a small smile. "Yeah...just hard to keep that momentum going, you know?"

JJ took a deep breath, looking thoughtful. "I get it, too. I feel like I'm always one slip-up away from messing everything up. My mom's proud of me for being here, but she's still worried. Thinks I might go back to hanging with the wrong crowd."

Dre, usually one of the more reserved ones in the group, spoke up. "For me, it's temptation. Like, my friends from before...they keep hitting me up, saying I've changed, that I'm forgetting where I come from. Part of me knows they're wrong, but it's tough when they're the ones who used to have my back."

The room fell silent, the weight of their struggles hanging in the air. Each of them had made strides, yet they were still haunted by the pressures of their environments and their past choices.

"Listen," Ben said, his voice firm but gentle, "you're all here because you want more for yourselves, and that's huge. But change takes time, and setbacks are part of the process. It's about finding a way to keep moving forward, even when it feels like the world's trying to pull you back."

Izzy, wanting to help lighten the mood, added with a smile, "Hey, maybe we could study together more. I mean, I helped JJ, and he's been doing better. We could have, like, a study squad."

Terry nodded, jumping in. "Yeah, I'd be down for that. I'm actually pretty good at science, so maybe I could help anyone struggling there."

X glanced around, surprised but appreciative of the idea. "Honestly, that sounds good. I didn't think I'd have people who'd actually want to help me with school stuff."

Ben smiled, pride filling his chest as he watched them support each other. They were becoming more than just a group of kids in a mentorship program; they were a team, looking out for one another in a way that would carry them forward.

"Let's make it official, then," Ben said with a grin. "You're not just learning firefighting skills here. You're building something bigger—a family, a support system. I'm proud of each of you, and I want you to keep pushing, keep challenging each other."

The boys looked around, nodding in agreement. The station felt like a safe haven, a place where they could share their hopes and struggles openly. And for the first time, they realized they weren't fighting their battles alone.

Chapter XVI

The following week, the boys arrived at the station for what Ben called a "crucial challenge." Today, they would be split into teams, tasked with coordinating a simulated rescue and fire suppression in a two-story training building. Each team would have specific roles: one group was responsible for finding and "rescuing" a dummy trapped in the building, while the other focused on containing the fire and ensuring the path to the exit remained clear.

As the boys suited up, they exchanged nervous glances, but there was an excitement in the air too. This was a step up—a real test of everything they'd been learning. Ben noticed the tension and addressed them with a firm but reassuring tone.

"Today's exercise isn't just about the rescue," he explained, looking each of them in the eye. "It's about communication, focus, and staying calm under pressure. You've got to trust each other. I know each of you has strengths to bring to this, so lean on each other. Now, let's get out there and show me what you've got."

JJ and Dre, who had been working closely together for weeks, were paired with Terry on the rescue team. They'd have to navigate darkened, narrow hallways to reach the "victim," while the rest of the boys—Izzy, Kal, X, and AJ—would handle the fire containment, keeping the path safe.

As the drill started, JJ took the lead, shouting directions over his shoulder as he guided Dre and Terry down the first set of stairs. The building was hazy, and even though it wasn't real smoke, the limited visibility gave the exercise a serious edge.

"Watch your step!" JJ called out as he crouched low, keeping his breathing steady. "We're almost there!"

Behind him, Terry stumbled slightly, but Dre caught his arm, steadying him. "You good?" Dre asked, his voice concerned.

"Yeah, thanks, man," Terry replied, giving a grateful nod. "Just got to stay focused."

Meanwhile, on the fire containment team, Izzy was carefully directing the others. His calm, analytical approach kept everyone focused. He called out measurements for hose positioning, and Kal listened intently, surprised by how much he respected Izzy's instructions.

"Kal, keep that water flow steady here," Izzy instructed, gesturing toward a specific area that simulated a blaze. "AJ, stay close. If we need to move, we do it fast."

X watched Izzy's precision with admiration, realizing for the first time that he wasn't the only one who had something to prove. They were all fighting their own battles, trying to rise above expectations, both from others and from themselves.

Back in the building, JJ finally spotted the dummy in the corner of a room. "Got him!" he yelled to Dre and Terry.

Together, they carefully hoisted the dummy up, working as a unit to carry it through the narrow, obstacle-laden corridors back toward the exit. As they approached, the fire containment team was there to ensure a clear path, their hoses strategically placed to "control" the mock blaze.

When they finally made it out of the building, sweaty but triumphant, the boys high-fived and congratulated each other. Ben was waiting, clapping proudly.

"Excellent work, team," he said, beaming at each of them. "You stayed calm, communicated well, and looked out for each other. That's what this is all about."

As they sat down to catch their breath, Ben gave them time to cool down, but he could sense there was more on their minds. After a few minutes, he leaned forward, encouraging them to open up.

"Let's check in. How's everything going outside of here?" Ben asked, watching each of their faces for a response.

Kal spoke up first, still energized from the drill. "Honestly, this...this helps a lot. I mean, school's still tough, and I'm barely passing, but being here makes me feel like I'm actually good at something, you know?"

Izzy nodded, a proud smile on his face. "Kal, you're a quick learner here. And don't worry about school, man. We can keep working on that together. Remember that math help we talked about? I got you."

Kal grinned, nodding gratefully. "I'd appreciate that, Izzy. Thanks."

JJ sighed, leaning back in his seat. "I feel like I'm doing okay, but it's hard to keep my head in the game all the time. My mom's proud, but every time I'm out of her sight, she still thinks I might mess up."

Dre nodded in understanding. "Yeah, I get that, man. My old friends are still hitting me up, acting like I've changed for the worse. Sometimes, it's tough ignoring their calls, especially when I'm walking home alone and they're right there."

AJ chimed in, his tone a bit more hopeful. "I feel the same sometimes, but I've been talking to my uncle more, and he keeps telling me how proud he is that I'm here. That keeps me going, even on rough days."

X, who had been listening quietly, finally spoke up, his voice calm but resolute. "You guys know I was close to giving up on school altogether before this. Now, it's still hard, but I want to finish. For the first time, I feel like I actually have something to look forward to. But man, it's a fight every day."

Terry, usually the quieter one, added his voice, surprising the group. "I struggle with feeling like I'm not good enough sometimes. But when we're here, when we're doing this...it feels like I can finally believe I'm capable."

The group fell silent for a moment, letting Terry's words sink in. They all understood that feeling—that quiet doubt that lingered even when they were making progress. Ben, watching their faces, decided to give them some words of encouragement.

"You've all come a long way," he said softly. "This program isn't just about firefighting. It's about showing yourselves that you're capable, that you have value, and that you're stronger than any doubt or past mistake."

Ben's words hit home, and the boys nodded in agreement, determination shining in their eyes. They were a team, brothers who'd begun this journey together, and they weren't about to let each other down.

The training session had ended, but the bonds they were building here—through shared struggles and small victories—were just beginning to take root.

Chapter XVII

The boys had been buzzing with excitement ever since Ben told them they could leave school early for the afternoon. They were heading to an elementary school across town to help with a fire safety demonstration, and it felt like a big deal for them. It was a chance to finally show that they were trustworthy and responsible. Each boy had a specific job to do. Some were going to teach the younger kids about the important steps of "stop, drop, and roll," while others would explain what a fire escape plan looked like. This was their opportunity to step up and be positive role models, showing the younger kids how to stay safe.

When Ben arrived at the station to pick them up, he quickly looked around to count the boys. But then he noticed something was off—one boy was missing. "Where's Dre?" he asked, glancing around. The other boys shifted uncomfortably, sharing nervous looks with one another.

"I don't know. He wasn't in school today," Izzy said quietly, staring at the ground.

Ben's expression changed, becoming more serious. "Alright. If anyone hears from him, let me know. But right now, you boys have a job to do, and we can't let Dre's absence distract us." On the way to the elementary school, the truck felt quieter than usual. As they drove, everyone wondered what was going on with Dre. For some of the boys, this wasn't the first time a friend had suddenly gone missing. They all knew the streets could pull people in, but this time felt different. Dre had worked hard to turn his life around and be part of this group. The uneasy feeling of his absence settled around them.

When they finally arrived at the elementary school, they saw the younger kids lined up outside, eagerly waiting to see the teens step out of Ben's truck. Each boy took their position at their assigned station. Once they started talking to the kids, the nerves they had began to fade away. Even Khalil, who usually kept up a tough front, found himself enjoying the curious questions the younger kids asked. Izzy, known for his math skills, had created a fun little game to teach the kids how to count the steps they would need to take to escape a fire. He was grinning from ear to ear as he led the kids in counting along with him, and they laughed the whole time.

Meanwhile, Terry was in his element. He was showing the kids how to "stop, drop, and roll." The younger kids eagerly mimicked his actions, falling over dramatically and giggling. X noticed how the kids looked at him with admiration, and he stood taller, filled with pride. This was a different experience—something that felt really good.

As the demonstration came to an end, the principal of the elementary school walked up to the boys to thank them. "You boys are doing something incredible here," she said warmly. "These kids really look up to you." She handed each of them a certificate of appreciation, marking a moment for many of them, as it was the first time they had received any kind of recognition.

On the ride back, their thoughts wandered back to Dre. They had been so focused on the demonstration that his absence had slipped to the back of their minds, but now it weighed heavily on them. Ben decided to pull the truck over for a moment. He turned in his seat to face the boys, his expression serious.

"Listen, I don't know what's going on with Dre," he said, "but I need you to remember that every choice you make shapes your future. While you can't control everything in life, you can control the path you choose to walk."

Just then, Ben's phone buzzed. He picked it up, and his face changed. Taking a shaky breath, he turned back to the boys, his expression grim. "Dre's been shot," he said softly.

A heavy silence fell in the truck as the news sank in. Some of the boys sat there in shock, while others lowered their heads, struggling to come to terms with what they had just heard. It felt unreal, like they were stuck in a nightmare they couldn't escape. Just hours before, they had been laughing and discussing what they would say to Dre when he returned. Now, they faced the frightening reality that they might not ever see him again.

"Is...is he okay?" Khalil asked, his voice barely a whisper as he searched the faces of his friends.

Ben swallowed hard, feeling the weight of the moment. "I don't know yet. But this is exactly what I've been trying to protect you all from. This is why you're in this program—to give you another choice, another chance to step away from that life."

As they drove back in silence, each boy grappled with the weight of what had happened. They'd known the risks of their old lives, but somehow, it felt different now that one of their own was lying in a hospital bed—or worse.

Back at the station, Ben gathered the boys around, looking each one in the eye. "This is why we're doing this. You all have potential—more than you know. Don't let this pull you back in. Let it push you forward. Dre would want that for you."

The boys nodded solemnly, the weight of Dre's absence pressing heavily on them. They had a lot to think about, and for the first time, they truly understood that their choices mattered.

Chapter XVIII

The news felt like a heavy punch to the gut for the boys. Dre was gone. He had been trying so hard to leave the streets behind him, hoping for a better life. But the brutal truth was that the very people he had once called friends couldn't handle his attempts to escape. They set him up, driven by jealousy of his efforts to break free from the life they all knew too well. The violence that took him away had ripped through their group, leaving them with the harsh reality of losing one of their own.

Ben had stumbled upon the news the night before, and since then, he hadn't managed to sleep at all. He understood that today's session had to be different—this was not the time for drills or exercises. What the boys needed most was a safe place to grieve, to talk about their feelings, and to know that they were understood. When they finally arrived, the usual buzz of energy that filled the air was absent, replaced instead by a heavy silence that spoke volumes of their collective grief.

They formed a circle, each taking their place on the floor, their eyes weighed down by the sorrow they all felt. Ben took a deep breath, trying to gather his thoughts before he spoke. His voice came out gentle but firm, carrying a sense of compassion that filled the room. "I know what you're feeling right now... and I know it's a lot. Losing Dre hurts deeply. He was one of us. And I want each of you to know that it's okay to feel however you're feeling."

For a moment, the room sat in silence, the weight of Ben's words hanging there. Finally, Isaiah couldn't hold back any longer. "It's not fair, man! Dre was trying. He was putting in the work. And they just... they didn't even give him a chance." His voice cracked as he expressed the frustration that everyone was feeling.

Khalil, his face tight with tension, nodded in agreement. "He wanted to be better. And they couldn't stand it." His hands were clenched into tight fists resting on his knees. "He didn't deserve that. He was fighting for a better life."

Terrence, who normally kept to himself, spoke up quietly, his voice barely above a whisper. "I thought... maybe if we worked hard enough, we could get out. But now...what if we're all just fooling ourselves?" The other boys shifted uncomfortably, the fear of their reality echoing through the room. What if despite all their efforts, the streets would still pull them back? It was a dark thought that none of them wanted to confront.

Ben saw the doubt creeping into their eyes, a shadow that threatened to consume them. He knew he had to guide them through this moment of despair. "Listen, I won't pretend that this world isn't harsh," he said, looking each boy in the eye. "But you have to remember, Dre didn't go down because he was trying to change. He went down because people were threatened by his strength. And that strength—his choice to change—is something they can never take from you unless you allow it."

Izzy wiped his eyes, frustration mixing with grief as he spoke. "It's just hard, you know? We're here, we're trying, but...out there, it's different. People see us, and they don't care about any of this." He waved his hand around the room, indicating their safe haven. "They just see who they think we used to be."

Jeremiah, his voice shaky but filled with determination, added, "I feel like...we need to stick together, now more than ever. Dre might be gone, but...we can't let this stop us. I think it'd be a waste if we let what happened to him make us give up." The boys nodded, their heads bowed, letting Jeremiah's words sink in. Ben watched as their shared pain began to shift, transforming into something that resembled a newfound resolve.

Khalil cleared his throat, his tone soft yet steady. "We need to honor him, you know? Make sure he didn't try to get out for nothing." Ben leaned in closer, the mood in the room shifting with a sense of purpose. "Exactly. You boys are on a path that Dre believed in. And if you let his loss push you off that path, then you let those who hurt him win."

Xavier, who had been quiet the entire time, finally lifted his head. His voice was heavy with sorrow as he spoke. "I've been thinking...maybe I should quit school. Just get a job, do something safe, something out of the way. But that's not what Dre would want, is it?" Agreement murmured through the group, and a subtle shift began to take place. Izzy looked around, his face now set with determination.

"Maybe we can help each other. I keep telling you guys that I'm good at math. I can tutor if anyone needs it. And whatever else you guys got, let's start bringing it here. School, goals, staying out of trouble—we help each other through it."

Jeremiah nodded, his face softening as he considered Izzy's words. "I don't know what I want yet, but I know I don't want to go back to where I was."

Isaiah added, his voice firm and resolute, "And if any of us starts slipping, we say something. No one's on their own here." The boys understood that they had to stick together, to rise from their grief and honor Dre's memory by moving forward on the path he believed they could take.

Ben could see the resolve solidifying in each of them, a sense of purpose growing out of the loss they felt. This was what Dre would have wanted, for them to keep pushing forward, even when it seemed impossible.

"Boys, if you take one thing away from today, let it be this," Ben said, his voice unwavering. "You are stronger together. You can support each other and lift each other up. And I'm here for you, every step of the way."

For the first time since Dre's death, a glimmer of hope appeared in their eyes. They didn't leave that day with all the answers, but they left with something more powerful: the understanding that they were not alone. As they walked out of the station, each one carried a piece of Dre's memory with them, promising to carry forward the path he had started.

Chapter XIX

The fire station had been transformed. The walls were lined with photos of Dre, moments captured during training sessions, and the laughs and jokes they had shared. It was a night meant to celebrate him—the Dre they all knew, the one who could make anyone laugh, even on the toughest days.

As people gathered, the boys took a moment to look around at the crowd. The community room was filled with friends, family, and people who had come to respect Dre. They had all come together to share in his memory.

Ben stepped up first, his voice calm but full of warmth. "Thank you all for being here. Tonight is about celebrating Dre and honoring his spirit." He paused, looking at the boys. "Dre was a fighter. He taught us all to push harder, even on days when it wasn't easy. And I know he'd want us to remember him with smiles."

JJ held the microphone next. "Dre was like that—always challenging us." He grinned, his eyes drifting to a photo of Dre with his arm around his shoulder, both of them laughing. "He was the first one to jump into anything. One time, he convinced me to race him on the obstacle course, and he left me in the dust." JJ chuckled, wiping a tear from his eye. "He just always made me want to do better, you know?"

Xavier, usually more reserved, stepped forward. "Dre had this way of getting you to do stuff you didn't think you could." He smiled slightly. "He got me to do push-ups with him at 5 a.m. once. Said if he was getting up that early, I had no excuse. Next thing I knew, I was out there with him, freezing but laughing the whole time."

Izzy stepped up, looking thoughtful. "Dre didn't care if we messed up—he'd just laugh it off and say, 'we're gonna be better than this tomorrow.' And somehow, you'd believe him."

"Yeah," AJ said, nodding. "Dre could always get us moving. And it wasn't just about doing drills or exercises. He'd make you want to stick around after and talk, just hanging out, making jokes." AJ laughed, adding, "I swear he could make anything sound like an adventure."

Kal's voice was quiet but strong. "Dre made me feel like I wasn't alone. Even when things were hard, he'd be there, making sure you knew he had your back. One time, I was ready to walk away from this whole thing, but he said, 'We got this, Kal. We're all in this together.' I still hear him saying that sometimes."

Terry took a deep breath before speaking. "Dre... he didn't leave anyone out. He'd always look out for me, and make sure I had a place in everything we did. If I didn't say anything for a while, he'd nudge me and say, 'Hey, we want to hear from you too, Terry.' He just knew how to make you feel like you mattered."

As they spoke, the room filled with laughter and nods of recognition. Dre wasn't just a friend to them; he was a brother. Someone who had shown them the kind of strength they all wanted to have.

JJ stepped forward one last time. He reached out, holding the microphone with both hands, and his voice softened. "Dre, this is for you, man. We're going to keep going, just like you would've wanted us to." He glanced at the candle they'd set up at the center of the room. "You're still with us, and we're going to make you proud."

The boys stood together in a circle, each of them quiet, reflecting. And in that moment, they made a silent promise to themselves—and to Dre—to keep on this path, for him and for each other.

Chapter XX

The boys gathered at the fire station as usual, sensing something different in the air. Today, there was a shift in the routine, and they quickly noticed a presence among the firefighters who stood nearby, nodding encouragingly in their direction.

Ben approached them with a warm smile. "Alright, fellas, today we have a special visitor. Chief Lewis is here, and he wanted to come down and chat with you all."

As the boys straightened up, Chief Lewis—a tall, imposing figure with a commanding yet kind demeanor—stepped forward. He gave a nod, his eyes warm and sincere.

"Good afternoon, gentlemen," he began. "I've been hearing about the incredible work you all have been putting in here. Thought it was about time I came down to meet you young men face to face."

JJ, still shaken by Dre's absence, spoke up with a respectful but quiet tone. "Thank you, Chief.

We're trying... some days are harder than others."

Chief Lewis nodded, understanding the weight in JJ's words. "I can only imagine. I know it hasn't been easy, especially with Dre's passing." He paused, looking at each of them. "I want to commend each one of you for showing up, and for continuing to put in the work even when it's hard. Coming back after a loss like that isn't something everyone can do."

The boys looked around at each other, a mixture of sadness and resilience in their faces. Izzy spoke up, his voice tinged with determination. "It's what Dre would have wanted. He was trying to turn things around, just like us."

Chief Lewis nodded solemnly. "That's exactly it. And in honoring that memory, you're not just doing this for yourselves but for him too. Loss can either set us back or push us forward, and from what I see here today, you all are choosing to keep moving forward."

Terry, who'd been struggling silently, glanced down, then back up, his voice barely a murmur. "Sometimes I wonder if I even deserve to be here... you know, after everything."

The Chief leaned in slightly, his gaze steady. "Son, none of us are perfect. Life doesn't always give us easy answers or second chances, but it's what we do when we get an opportunity like this that counts. You're here, you're showing up, and you're putting in the work. That's what matters."

Xavier, encouraged by the Chief's words, asked, "Did you ever feel like turning back?"

The Chief's eyes softened. "More times than I can count. Starting out, I had plenty of days when I wanted to quit. I had my struggles, too, and plenty of doubts. But over time, I realized that my choices mattered—not just to me, but to those around me. It's the same with you all. Every time you choose to show up here, you're making a choice that impacts others, not just yourselves."

Kal, still grappling with old friends and new choices, leaned forward. "It's hard to keep going when some people just expect us to fail."

"Believe me, I know that feeling," Chief Lewis said with a nod. "But remember, you're building something right now—a foundation that will change how others see you and, more importantly, how you see yourselves. It takes time, but it's worth it."

Ben, who had been quietly observing, spoke up, "I couldn't agree more. The commitment you've all shown, especially with everything you've been through, speaks volumes."

The Chief turned to address the group, a look of pride on his face. "You're part of a team now, and that's a powerful thing. Keep looking out for each other, keep pushing forward, and know that you have people rooting for you."

JJ leaned back, a small grin appearing. "Guess we better keep showing up, then."

The Chief chuckled, his voice warm. "That's the spirit. I'll be keeping an eye on you all, and remember, you have a whole department behind you."

As the boys moved back to their training exercises, they carried with them a renewed sense of purpose. Dre's memory was alive among them, pushing them to keep going, to keep showing up. And with Chief Lewis's words ringing in their ears, they felt ready to tackle whatever lay ahead, knowing they were part of something bigger than themselves.

Chapter XXI

The fire station hummed with a mix of nerves and excitement as the boys arrived early for the Firefighter 1 exam. For months, they had been practicing skills and taking in fire safety knowledge, drilling everything from gear checks to rescue maneuvers. Today, they'd find out if their hard work would pay off.

JJ adjusted his jacket, looking around at his friends. "Alright, I haven't been this nervous since my first middle school test."

Kal grinned, nudging him. "Same here. But we've got this. We trained for this, right?"

Ben walked up with a stack of exam materials and instructions. "Alright, guys. This is what all your effort's been building toward. Remember, the Firefighter 1 exam isn't just about being fast. It's about focus, precision, and thinking clearly under pressure."

The Chief joined them briefly, resting a hand on JJ's shoulder. "You boys have come far. Whatever happens today, just know we're proud of you."

The written exam was up first, covering the technical knowledge of fire safety, protocols, and equipment. They had an hour to complete it, and the silence in the room grew intense. Questions on hose pressure, safety procedures, fire chemistry, and handling hazardous materials popped up on the page. The boys glanced at each other occasionally, each one deeply focused, but Izzy in particular seemed calm, jotting down answers with steady confidence. The tutoring sessions with him had paid off; even Terry, who'd struggled with the more technical aspects, found himself recalling Izzy's explanations on safety protocols.

When the written portion wrapped up, they filed into the training ground for the practical exercises. Each boy took deep breaths, mentally preparing as they lined up for the first task.

Ben gave them a final pep talk, looking each of them in the eyes. "You know these drills inside out. Remember, it's not just about speed—it's about handling things smoothly and accurately. Trust yourselves, and don't rush."

The first test was the gear-up drill. They had sixty seconds to suit up completely, getting all equipment on securely. JJ's hands shook as he grabbed his helmet, but Xavier flashed him a thumbs-up. "You got this, JJ. Just like every other drill."

With that, JJ took a deep breath and refocused. The timer began, and he moved quickly, his hands more confident with each step. Next to him, Kal finished a few seconds ahead, flashing a grin. They both completed it under the limit, feeling a rush of relief.

Next came the hose drill, requiring each of them to connect hoses and direct the water with precision. This exercise reminded them of Dre, who'd put extra hours into mastering it before his passing. Each boy felt Dre's absence as they went through the task, but they pushed on with renewed determination. This one was for him.

Then came the ladder climb and victim drag. This was the toughest section, with obstacles that required both strength and endurance. The boys pushed themselves, breathing hard as they dragged weighted dummies and navigated low-visibility obstacles. They encouraged each other along the way, shouting out cheers and motivating one another through the final stretch.

Finally, they all completed the drill, drenched in sweat but with pride glowing on their faces.

Ben and the Chief gathered them together, grinning with admiration.

The Chief looked over at the boys, his voice full of pride. "You've proven yourselves. We'll tally up the scores, but I can already tell that you're all true firefighters in spirit."

After a short wait, Ben called them back. "Results are in. All of you passed—except for one," he said, glancing toward Kal with an empathetic look.

Kal's face fell, his shoulders slumping. "I missed it?"

Ben nodded, then added, "But barely. Just a couple of points on the practical. It's nothing you can't overcome. You'll get a retake in a couple of weeks, and I'll be here to help you prepare."

Immediately, the other boys gathered around Kal, their faces filled with determination. "You're almost there, man," Izzy encouraged, clapping him on the shoulder. "We're all gonna help you nail this."

Kal managed a small smile, grateful for his friend's support. "Thanks, guys. I'll do it right next time."

As they left the training area, each boy felt a renewed sense of purpose and pride. Passing this test wasn't just an achievement; it was a reminder of how far they'd come and a promise of what was still ahead.

Ben and Chief Lewis exchanged a proud look, witnessing the camaraderie and strength in this group of boys who had become more than just teammates—they were family.

Chapter XXII

As the weeks flew by, the atmosphere at the fire station became charged with determination as the boys returned day after day, eager to help their friend Kal with his training. Each member of the group rallied around Kal, motivated to see him succeed in the practical portion of the Firefighter 1 exam. This was a new experience for Kal, who found himself in the spotlight as the focus of their support. His friends were not only there to encourage him but also to challenge him at every turn, ensuring he was fully prepared for the big day ahead.

With the day of Kal's retake approaching, the boys gathered at the fire station for an extra training session, where Ben took the lead and organized a demanding drill for the entire group. The session transcended Kal's personal journey; it became a collective effort to sharpen their own skills while supporting Kal. They dedicated hours to working through each part of the practical test, practicing various drills, and taking turns running through mock exercises to simulate the test conditions.

During one of these drills, Xavier took a moment to lean over Kal as he set up the hose connection. He carefully adjusted Kal's stance, ensuring that every detail was correct. "Remember, man, every move counts," he reminded Kal, his voice steady and encouraging. "Don't let the pressure get to you." Kal nodded, adjusting his gloves with resolve, embodying the determination of his friends and himself.

The boys designed numerous drills and took turns standing by to watch Kal perform. They gently urged him to work at a quicker pace, guiding him to handle the equipment with more confidence and precision while reminding him to maintain control over each action. Their teamwork made the atmosphere electric, each of them eager to see Kal succeed. Once they wrapped up the intense training session, the group moved to the fire station lounge where they gathered together. The sound of their laughter filled the room, blending with an undercurrent of anticipation that hung in the air. Ben, who had been silently observing their dedicated practice, approached them with a genuine smile. "You guys have been doing great," he announced, looking directly at Kal. "And Kal, you're ready. I can see it."

Kal's expression brightened at Ben's words. "Thanks, Ben. I really appreciate all of you pushing me. I honestly didn't think I'd make it this far."

Terry gave him a supportive pat on the back, reinforcing their bond. "You'll nail it, Kal. And when you do, we're throwing a little celebration. We have to celebrate every victory."

Kal's mood lifted even more as he smiled back at Terry. "I'll hold you to that, Terry," he replied, feeling the weight of his worries lighten.

Finally, the long-awaited day of Kal's exam retake arrived, and his friends made sure to come out to support him. Ben was there to supervise, guiding Kal methodically through each step of the process. As he moved through the tasks, Kal felt his nerves fade, replaced by a growing sense of focus and determination. He engaged fully with the skills his friends had taught him, centering his thoughts on achieving the goal he had set for himself.

When Kal completed the last task, he looked up, breathless with excitement, to see his friends erupting in applause and cheers. Ben approached him, his face beaming with pride. "Congratulations, Kal. You passed."

The fire station erupted in joyous cheers, and the boys lifted Kal into the air in celebration. The relief and happiness on his face were unmistakable. He had achieved his goal, and he had done it surrounded by the unwavering support of his friends.

Afterward, they gathered for a small celebration, enjoying sodas and snacks together. Each boy took a moment to share encouraging words, reminiscing about the challenges and victories they had experienced as a team.

Izzy raised his drink high. "To Kal, and to all of us for sticking together. We're almost at the finish line, boys."

Laughter and the sound of clinking bottles filled the room as they celebrated Kal's achievement and the strong bond they had built together during their shared journey.

Chapter XXIII

The fire station was buzzing with excitement. Families, friends, firefighters, and EMTs filled the space, their faces lit with pride and anticipation. Balloons in red and white floated near the ceiling, and a long banner reading "Congratulations, Firefighter Trainees!" stretched across the wall.

Ben stood near the front, a smile tugging at the corner of his mouth as he watched the boys, each one dressed in a crisp blue fire station t-shirt and looking ready for their big moment. The months of training, the struggles, and the triumphs had all led to this day, and he couldn't be prouder.

"Man, I can't believe this is really happening," Isaiah whispered, his eyes scanning the crowd until he found his family. They waved at him, faces beaming.

"I know," Kal replied, his voice filled with excitement. "All those late nights studying and running drills... It's actually paying off."

Xavier gave them a nudge, grinning. "We earned this, y'all. Every single one of us."

The crowd quieted as the fire chief, a respected figure in the community, stepped up to the podium. His deep voice carried warmth as he began to speak.

"Today, we honor seven young men who took a chance on themselves and worked hard to earn their place here. They've shown dedication, courage, and perseverance. I think it's safe to say that each of you has grown in ways you might not even realize yet." He looked at the boys, his expression full of pride. "You're an inspiration—not only to each other but to all of us."

The boys glanced at each other, soaking in the words, feeling both proud and a little overwhelmed.

The chief continued, "When you started, you didn't just join a program. You joined a family. And in our family, we look out for each other, lift each other up, and—when things get tough—we stick together. I've watched you all go through challenges, and today you stand here as graduates because you've proven you're ready."

Ben stepped forward then, holding a small stack of certificates. "Alright, it's time for the official part." He looked each boy in the eye as he called their names.

"Jeremiah, come on up."

JJ, grinning from ear to ear, walked up, his family cheering as he accepted his certificate from Ben. They shook hands, and JJ gave him a quick, grateful nod before stepping back.

"Xavier"

X's parents clapped and whooped as he went up. Ben gave him a firm handshake, and Dre held the certificate like it was a badge of honor. One by one, each of the boys took their turn— Isaiah, Khalil, Andre, and finally, Terrence. By the end, all seven boys stood at the front of the room, certificates in hand, faces glowing with pride. They glanced at each other, unable to hide their joy.

The chief raised his hands. "Now, I have a little surprise for each of you. These aren't just certificates. Each one of you has earned the title of honorary volunteer firefighter, which means from now on, you're part of our team."

The boys' eyes widened, surprised, and deeply moved. The crowd erupted into applause, and a few tears were shed among the family members, who couldn't be prouder.

Ben walked over, placing a hand on each boy's shoulder as he spoke. "Today, you've all earned the respect and trust of this community. Remember Dre, and how he inspired you to keep going. He'd be proud. And now, you'll always have a place here. This is your family now, too."

The boys stood in silence, taking in the weight of his words. For some of them, it was the first time they'd ever felt truly part of something. They looked out over the crowd, at their families and the firefighters who had become mentors and friends. It was overwhelming but in the best way possible.

JJ cleared his throat, trying to keep his emotions in check. "Thank you, Coach. Thanks for believing in us when no one else did."

The other boys nodded, each one echoing JJ's sentiment in their own way, with pats on the back, hugs, and handshakes. They didn't need to say much; the moment spoke for itself.

As the ceremony ended, Ben gathered them in for a final huddle. "No matter where life takes you, remember this feeling, and remember what you've accomplished here. This is just the beginning."

They all nodded, holding onto the moment, the weight of their accomplishment settling in. They were different from the boys who had first entered the program; they were stronger, wiser, and bound together by experiences that had changed them.

As they broke from the huddle, they each knew one thing for certain: they'd never be alone again. They were family, now and forever.

Chapter XXIV

A week had passed since graduation, but the fire station still felt like home to the boys. They returned that Friday evening, as they always had, to find Ben waiting for them in the back room. This time, however, the mood was different—this wasn't a training session, and there were no drills planned. It was a moment of reflection, closure, and gratitude.

Ben looked around at each of the young men, a deep pride shining in his eyes. "Look at you all," he said, his voice a bit rough around the edges. "Months ago, you were a group of strangers with a lot to prove. And now? You're brothers, each with the potential to make a real difference."

Isaiah nodded, speaking up. "Coach, I don't think any of us could have imagined this day. I mean, you taught us what it means to really be a team, to believe in each other."

The others agreed, their faces alight with memories of the journey that had brought them here. They shared stories of moments that had stuck with them: the first firehouse drill when none of them could stop tripping over hoses, the brutal yet rewarding fitness challenges, and the endless reminders from Ben to "show up and give it everything."

JJ looked at the group, grinning as he reminisced. "Remember the time Kal almost knocked over the whole equipment rack during drills?" he laughed, and the others joined in, remembering Kal's horrified expression at the sight of everything falling down.

Kal shrugged, smiling sheepishly. "Hey, at least I didn't get soaked trying to attach the fire hose to the wrong hydrant," he shot back, glancing at Andre, who laughed even harder.

Ben chuckled along with them, shaking his head. "It's these moments," he said, his voice softening, "that makes you more than just firefighters. They make you men who can trust each other, who can lean on each other when life gets rough."

The room fell quiet as they considered his words, each boy reflecting on what Ben's mentorship had meant to them. He wasn't just a coach or a mentor; he had become a father figure, a guide, someone they could depend on.

Dre's absence hung in the air, but instead of silence, the boys filled the room with stories that kept his memory alive. "Dre used to push me harder than anyone," Xavier said, a mix of sorrow and pride in his voice. "Every time I wanted to quit, he was right there, telling me I'd regret it if I didn't finish strong."

They each shared a memory of Dre, honoring him not in silence but with laughter, stories, and a bond that only deepened through their shared loss. In a way, Dre had brought them even closer, inspiring them to keep pushing forward.

Ben watched, letting the boys speak until there were no more words left. Then, clearing his throat, he gathered them in for a final huddle. "I want each of you to remember this," he began, his voice low and serious. "You've got what it takes to make it through anything life throws your way. You're part of something bigger now, and you've all got people here rooting for you. Don't forget that."

The boys looked around, nodding. It was a promise—one they made to themselves and to each other.

As they straightened up, Ben handed each of them a small, polished plaque with their name engraved on it. Beneath each name was the title "Honorary Firefighter" and the date they'd completed the program. Each boy accepted the plaque, feeling the weight of what it symbolized.

After a moment, Ben addressed them one last time. "This doesn't have to be goodbye. You're welcome here anytime—whether to volunteer, to help out, or just to hang around. And I expect to see each of you back, stronger and smarter than before."

JJ stepped forward, looking at Ben, trying to find the right words. "Coach... thank you. For everything. We won't let you down."

Ben clapped JJ on the shoulder, then looked around at the others. "I know you won't," he said with a smile. "You've already done more than I could ever ask for."

As the boys left the fire station that night, they knew it wasn't truly an ending. It was the start of something new, with friendships that would last a lifetime and a purpose that had given each of them a reason to rise above.

And as they walked down the road from the station, their heads held high, they felt a new confidence—one they'd earned together, one they'd carry with them no matter where life took them next.